Acclaim for GISH JEN*'s*

WHO'S IRISH?

"Gish Jen's stories are keenly observed moments in time, in which the characters' foibles predominate just long enough for an odd equilibrium to be established between their yearning and their movement toward small, unexpected moments of grace. In many of the stories the characters seem to be trying on their lives for size: discomfiting to observe, though at the same time, offering the reader a sadness convincingly tinged with humor."
　　　　　　　　　　　　　　　　　　　　　—Ann Beattie

"Jen's performance isn't a series of one-liners, but an elaborate balancing act: Chinese and American, painful and funny. . . . The result: an esthetic whole even greater than the sum of its entertaining parts."
　　　　　　　　　　　　　　　　　　　　　—*Newsweek*

"Biting and insightful. . . . It universalizes the experience of the 'hyphenated American' in a way that allows any person—white, black, yellow, purple or green—who ever has felt marginalized or rootless to see it as his or her own. . . . The product of a true craftswoman whose gifts transcend all cultural and ethnic labels."
　　　　　　　　　　　　　　　　　　　　　—*USA Today*

"Tender and funny . . . vibrant and courageous."
　　　　　　　　　　　　—*San Francisco Chronicle Book Review*

"Jen's quicksilver wit and devastating eye wryly capture the poignancy of American-style ambition on the ethnic fringe."
—*Mirabella*

"Jen's stories are amazingly compressed, and she studs them with perversely funny social disasters that explode like skillfully placed narrative land mines . . . her voice sings with authenticity."
—*Entertainment Weekly*

"Wonderful. . . . Gish Jen belongs with the best of them."
—*The Newark Star-Ledger*

GISH JEN

WHO'S IRISH?

Gish Jen grew up in Scarsdale, New York, and grad-uated from Harvard. Her work has appeared in *The New Yorker*, *The Atlantic Monthly*, and *The Best American Short Stories of the Century*. The author of two novels, *Typical American* and *Mona in the Promised Land*, she lives in Massachusetts with her husband and two children.

ALSO BY GISH JEN

Typical American

Mona in the Promised Land

WHO'S IRISH?

WHO'S IRISH?

STORIES

GISH JEN

VINTAGE CONTEMPORARIES

Vintage Books

A Division of Random House, Inc.

New York

FIRST VINTAGE CONTEMPORARIES EDITION, JUNE 2000

Copyright © 1999 by Gish Jen

All rights reserved under International and Pan-American Copyright Conventions. Published in the United States by Vintage Books, a division of Random House, Inc., New York, and simultaneously in Canada by Random House of Canada Limited, Toronto. Originally published in hardcover in the United States by Alfred A. Knopf, a division of Random House, Inc., New York, in 1999.

Vintage is a registered trademark and Vintage Contemporaries and colophon are trademarks of Random House, Inc.

Some of the stories in this collection were previously published as follows: "Who's Irish?" in *The New Yorker* (1998). • "The Water Faucet Vision" in *Nimrod* (1988) and also in *Best American Short Stories 1988.* • "Birthmates" in *Ploughshares* (1995), in *Best American Short Stories 1995,* and in *Best American Short Stories of the Century* (1999). • "Just Wait" in *Ploughshares* (1998). • "In the American Society" in *The Southern Review* (1986). • "Chin" in the collection *Shorts* (Granta Books, 1998).

Grateful acknowledgment is made to Sony/ATV Music Publishing for permission to reprint an excerpt from "Yellow Submarine," words and music by John Lennon and Paul McCartney, copyright © 1966 by Sony/ATV Tunes LLC., copyright renewed. All rights administered by Sony/ATV Music Publishing, 8 Music Square West, Nashville, TN 37203. All rights reserved. Reprinted by permission.

The Library of Congress has cataloged the Knopf edition as follows:
Jen, Gish.
Who's Irish? stories / by Gish Jen. — 1st ed.
p. cm.
1. United States—Social life and customs—20th century—Fiction.
2. Chinese American families—Fiction. 3. Chinese Americans—Fiction. I. Title.
PS3560.E474W48 1999
813'.54—dc21. 98-42801
CIP

Vintage ISBN: 0-375-70592-9

Author photograph © Jill Krementz

www.vintagebooks.com

Printed in the United States of America
10 9 8 7 6 5 4 3 2 1

For Luke,
bringer of light

CONTENTS

WHO'S IRISH?

WHO'S IRISH?

In China, people say mixed children are supposed to be smart, and definitely my granddaughter Sophie is smart. But Sophie is wild, Sophie is not like my daughter Natalie, or like me. I am work hard my whole life, and fierce besides. My husband always used to say he is afraid of me, and in our restaurant, busboys and cooks all afraid of me too. Even the gang members come for protection money, they try to talk to my husband. When I am there, they stay away. If they come by mistake, they pretend they are come to eat. They hide behind the menu, they order a lot of food. They talk about their mothers. Oh, my mother have some arthritis, need to take herbal medicine, they say. Oh, my mother getting old, her hair all white now.

I say, Your mother's hair used to be white, but since she dye it, it become black again. Why don't you go home once in a while and take a look? I tell them, Confucius say a filial son knows what color his mother's hair is.

My daughter is fierce too, she is vice president in the bank now. Her new house is big enough for everybody to have their own room, including me. But Sophie take after Natalie's husband's family, their name is Shea. Irish. I always thought Irish people are like Chinese people, work so hard on the railroad, but now I know why the Chinese beat the Irish. Of course, not all Irish are like the Shea family, of course not. My daughter tell me I should not say Irish this, Irish that.

Who's Irish?

How do you like it when people say the Chinese this, the Chinese that, she say.

You know, the British call the Irish heathen, just like they call the Chinese, she say.

You think the Opium War was bad, how would you like to live right next door to the British, she say.

And that is that. My daughter have a funny habit when she win an argument, she take a sip of something and look away, so the other person is not embarrassed. So I am not embarrassed. I do not call anybody anything either. I just happen to mention about the Shea family, an interesting fact: four brothers in the family, and not one of them work. The mother, Bess, have a job before she got sick, she was executive secretary in a big company. She is handle everything for a big shot, you would be surprised how complicated her job is, not just type this, type that. Now she is a nice woman with a clean house. But her boys, every one of them is on welfare, or so-called severance pay, or so-called disability pay. Something. They say they cannot find work, this is not the economy of the fifties, but I say, Even the black people doing better these days, some of them live so fancy, you'd be surprised. Why the Shea family have so much trouble? They are white people, they speak English. When I come to this country, I have no money and do not speak English. But my husband and I own our restaurant before he die. Free and clear, no mortgage. Of course, I understand I am just lucky, come from a country where the food is popular all over the world. I understand it is not the Shea family's fault they come from a country where everything is boiled. Still, I say.

She's right, we should broaden our horizons, say one brother, Jim, at Thanksgiving. Forget about the car business. Think about egg rolls.

Pad thai, say another brother, Mike. I'm going to make my fortune in pad thai. It's going to be the new pizza.

I say, You people too picky about what you sell. Selling egg rolls not good enough for you, but at least my husband and I can say, We made it. What can you say? Tell me. What can you say?

Everybody chew their tough turkey.

I especially cannot understand my daughter's husband John, who has no job but cannot take care of Sophie either. Because he is a man, he say, and that's the end of the sentence.

Plain boiled food, plain boiled thinking. Even his name is plain boiled: John. Maybe because I grew up with black bean sauce and hoisin sauce and garlic sauce, I always feel something is missing when my son-in-law talk.

But, okay: so my son-in-law can be man, I am baby-sitter. Six hours a day, same as the old sitter, crazy Amy, who quit. This is not so easy, now that I am sixty-eight, Chinese age almost seventy. Still, I try. In China, daughter take care of mother. Here it is the other way around. Mother help daughter, mother ask, Anything else I can do? Otherwise daughter complain mother is not supportive. I tell daughter, We do not have this word in Chinese, *supportive*. But my daughter too busy to listen, she has to go to meeting, she has to write memo while her husband go to the gym to be a man. My daughter say otherwise he will be depressed. Seems like all his life he has this trouble, depression.

No one wants to hire someone who is depressed, she say. It is important for him to keep his spirits up.

Beautiful wife, beautiful daughter, beautiful house, oven can clean itself automatically. No money left over, because only one income, but lucky enough, got the baby-sitter for free. If John lived in China, he would be very happy. But he is not happy. Even at the gym things go wrong. One day, he pull a muscle. Another day, weight room too crowded. Always something.

Until finally, hooray, he has a job. Then he feel pressure.

I need to concentrate, he say. I need to focus.

Who's Irish?

He is going to work for insurance company. Salesman job. A paycheck, he say, and at least he will wear clothes instead of gym shorts. My daughter buy him some special candy bars from the health-food store. They say THINK! on them, and are supposed to help John think.

John is a good-looking boy, you have to say that, especially now that he shave so you can see his face.

I am an old man in a young man's game, say John.

I will need a new suit, say John.

This time I am not going to shoot myself in the foot, say John.

Good, I say.

She means to be supportive, my daughter say. Don't start the send her back to China thing, because we can't.

Sophie is three years old American age, but already I see her nice Chinese side swallowed up by her wild Shea side. She looks like mostly Chinese. Beautiful black hair, beautiful black eyes. Nose perfect size, not so flat looks like something fell down, not so large looks like some big deal got stuck in wrong face. Everything just right, only her skin is a brown surprise to John's family. So brown, they say. Even John say it. She never goes in the sun, still she is that color, he say. Brown. They say, Nothing the matter with brown. They are just surprised. So brown. Nattie is not that brown, they say. They say, It seems like Sophie should be a color in between Nattie and John. Seems funny, a girl named Sophie Shea be brown. But she is brown, maybe her name should be Sophie Brown. She never go in the sun, still she is that color, they say. Nothing the matter with brown. They are just surprised.

The Shea family talk is like this sometimes, going around and around like a Christmas-tree train.

Maybe John is not her father, I say one day, to stop the train.

And sure enough, train wreck. None of the brothers ever say the word *brown* to me again.

Instead, John's mother, Bess, say, I hope you are not offended.

She say, I did my best on those boys. But raising four boys with no father is no picnic.

You have a beautiful family, I say.

I'm getting old, she say.

You deserve a rest, I say. Too many boys make you old.

I never had a daughter, she say. You have a daughter.

I have a daughter, I say. Chinese people don't think a daughter is so great, but you're right. I have a daughter.

I was never against the marriage, you know, she say. I never thought John was marrying down. I always thought Nattie was just as good as white.

I was never against the marriage either, I say. I just wonder if they look at the whole problem.

Of course you pointed out the problem, you are a mother, she say. And now we both have a granddaughter. A little brown granddaughter, she is so precious to me.

I laugh. A little brown granddaughter, I say. To tell you the truth, I don't know how she came out so brown.

We laugh some more. These days Bess need a walker to walk. She take so many pills, she need two glasses of water to get them all down. Her favorite TV show is about bloopers, and she love her bird feeder. All day long, she can watch that bird feeder, like a cat.

I can't wait for her to grow up, Bess say. I could use some female company.

Too many boys, I say.

Boys are fine, she say. But they do surround you after a while.

You should take a break, come live with us, I say. Lots of girls at our house.

Be careful what you offer, say Bess with a wink. Where I

come from, people mean for you to move in when they say a thing like that.

Nothing the matter with Sophie's outside, that's the truth. It is inside that she is like not any Chinese girl I ever see. We go to the park, and this is what she does. She stand up in the stroller. She take off all her clothes and throw them in the fountain.

Sophie! I say. Stop!

But she just laugh like a crazy person. Before I take over as baby-sitter, Sophie has that crazy-person sitter, Amy the guitar player. My daughter thought this Amy very creative—another word we do not talk about in China. In China, we talk about whether we have difficulty or no difficulty. We talk about whether life is bitter or not bitter. In America, all day long, people talk about creative. Never mind that I cannot even look at this Amy, with her shirt so short that her belly button showing. This Amy think Sophie should love her body. So when Sophie take off her diaper, Amy laugh. When Sophie run around naked, Amy say she wouldn't want to wear a diaper either. When Sophie go *shu-shu* in her lap, Amy laugh and say there are no germs in pee. When Sophie take off her shoes, Amy say bare feet is best, even the pediatrician say so. That is why Sophie now walk around with no shoes like a beggar child. Also why Sophie love to take off her clothes.

Turn around! say the boys in the park. Let's see that ass!

Of course, Sophie does not understand. Sophie clap her hands, I am the only one to say, No! This is not a game.

It has nothing to do with John's family, my daughter say. Amy was too permissive, that's all.

But I think if Sophie was not wild inside, she would not take off her shoes and clothes to begin with.

You never take off your clothes when you were little, I say. my Chinese friends had babies, I never saw one of them act wild like that.

Look, my daughter say. I have a big presentation tomorrow.

John and my daughter agree Sophie is a problem, but they don't know what to do.

You spank her, she'll stop, I say another day.

But they say, Oh no.

In America, parents not supposed to spank the child.

It gives them low self-esteem, my daughter say. And that leads to problems later, as I happen to know.

My daughter never have big presentation the next day when the subject of spanking come up.

I don't want you to touch Sophie, she say. No spanking, period.

Don't tell me what to do, I say.

I'm not telling you what to do, say my daughter. I'm telling you how I feel.

I am not your servant, I say. Don't you dare talk to me like that.

My daughter have another funny habit when she lose an argument. She spread out all her fingers and look at them, as if she like to make sure they are still there.

My daughter is fierce like me, but she and John think it is better to explain to Sophie that clothes are a good idea. This is not so hard in the cold weather. In the warm weather, it is very hard.

Use your words, my daughter say. That's what we tell Sophie. How about if you set a good example.

As if good example mean anything to Sophie. I am so fierce, the gang members who used to come to the restaurant all afraid of me, but Sophie is not afraid.

I say, Sophie, if you take off your clothes, no snack.

I say, Sophie, if you take off your clothes, no lunch.

, if you take off your clothes, no park.

we are stay home all day, and by the end of six
did not have one thing to eat. You never saw a child
that.

I m ... y! she cry when my daughter come home.

What's the matter, doesn't your grandmother feed you? My
daughter laugh.

No! Sophie say. She doesn't feed me anything!

My daughter laugh again. Here you go, she say.

She say to John, Sophie must be growing.

Growing like a weed, I say.

Still Sophie take off her clothes, until one day I spank her. Not
too hard, but she cry and cry, and when I tell her if she doesn't put
her clothes back on I'll spank her again, she put her clothes back
on. Then I tell her she is good girl, and give her some food to eat.
The next day we go to the park and, like a nice Chinese girl, she
does not take off her clothes.

She stop taking off her clothes, I report. Finally!

How did you do it? my daughter ask.

After twenty-eight years experience with you, I guess I learn
something, I say.

It must have been a phase, John say, and his voice is suddenly
like an expert.

His voice is like an expert about everything these days, now
that he carry a leather briefcase, and wear shiny shoes, and can go
shopping for a new car. On the company, he say. The company
will pay for it, but he will be able to drive it whenever he want.

A free car, he say. How do you like that.

It's good to see you in the saddle again, my daughter say. Some
of your family patterns are scary.

At least I don't drink, he say. He say, And I'm not the only one
with scary family patterns.

That's for sure, say my daughter.

. . .

Everyone is happy. Even I am happy, because there is more trouble with Sophie, but now I think I can help her Chinese side fight against her wild side. I teach her to eat food with fork or spoon or chopsticks, she cannot just grab into the middle of a bowl of noodles. I teach her not to play with garbage cans. Sometimes I spank her, but not too often, and not too hard.

Still, there are problems. Sophie like to climb everything. If there is a railing, she is never next to it. Always she is on top of it. Also, Sophie like to hit the mommies of her friends. She learn this from her playground best friend, Sinbad, who is four. Sinbad wear army clothes every day and like to ambush his mommy. He is the one who dug a big hole under the play structure, a foxhole he call it, all by himself. Very hardworking. Now he wait in the foxhole with a shovel full of wet sand. When his mommy come, he throw it right at her.

Oh, it's all right, his mommy say. You can't get rid of war games, it's part of their imaginative play. All the boys go through it.

Also, he like to kick his mommy, and one day he tell Sophie to kick his mommy too.

I wish this story is not true.

Kick her, kick her! Sinbad say.

Sophie kick her. A little kick, as if she just so happened was swinging her little leg and didn't realize that big mommy leg was in the way. Still I spank Sophie and make Sophie say sorry, and what does the mommy say?

Really, it's all right, she say. It didn't hurt.

After that, Sophie learn she can attack mommies in the playground, and some will say, Stop, but others will say, Oh, she didn't mean it, especially if they realize Sophie will be punished.

. . .

Who's Irish?

This is how, one day, bigger trouble come. The bigger trouble start when Sophie hide in the foxhole with that shovel full of sand. She wait, and when I come look for her, she throw it at me. All over my nice clean clothes.

Did you ever see a Chinese girl act this way?

Sophie! I say. Come out of there, say you're sorry.

But she does not come out. Instead, she laugh. Naaah, naah-na, naaa-naaa, she say.

I am not exaggerate: millions of children in China, not one act like this.

Sophie! I say. Now! Come out now!

But she know she is in big trouble. She know if she come out, what will happen next. So she does not come out. I am sixty-eight, Chinese age almost seventy, how can I crawl under there to catch her? Impossible. So I yell, yell, yell, and what happen? Nothing. A Chinese mother would help, but American mothers, they look at you, they shake their head, they go home. And, of course, a Chinese child would give up, but not Sophie.

I hate you! she yell. I hate you, Meanie!

Meanie is my new name these days.

Long time this goes on, long long time. The foxhole is deep, you cannot see too much, you don't know where is the bottom. You cannot hear too much either. If she does not yell, you cannot even know she is still there or not. After a while, getting cold out, getting dark out. No one left in the playground, only us.

Sophie, I say. How did you become stubborn like this? I am go home without you now.

I try to use a stick, chase her out of there, and once or twice I hit her, but still she does not come out. So finally I leave. I go outside the gate.

Bye-bye! I say. I'm go home now.

But still she does not come out and does not come out. Now it is dinnertime, the sky is black. I think I should maybe go get help, but how can I leave a little girl by herself in the playground? A bad man could come. A rat could come. I go back in to see what is happen to Sophie. What if she have a shovel and is making a tunnel to escape?

Sophie! I say.

No answer.

Sophie!

I don't know if she is alive. I don't know if she is fall asleep down there. If she is crying, I cannot hear her.

So I take the stick and poke.

Sophie! I say. I promise I no hit you. If you come out, I give you a lollipop.

No answer. By now I worried. What to do, what to do, what to do? I poke some more, even harder, so that I am poking and poking when my daughter and John suddenly appear.

What are you doing? What is going on? say my daughter.

Put down that stick! say my daughter.

You are crazy! say my daughter.

John wiggle under the structure, into the foxhole, to rescue Sophie.

She fell asleep, say John the expert. She's okay. That is one big hole.

Now Sophie is crying and crying.

Sophia, my daughter say, hugging her. Are you okay, peanut? Are you okay?

She's just scared, say John.

Are you okay? I say too. I don't know what happen, I say.

She's okay, say John. He is not like my daughter, full of questions. He is full of answers until we get home and can see by the lamplight.

Will you look at her? he yell then. What the hell happened?

Bruises all over her brown skin, and a swollen-up eye.

You are crazy! say my daughter. Look at what you did! You are crazy!

I try very hard, I say.

How could you use a stick? I told you to use your words!

She is hard to handle, I say.

She's three years old! You cannot use a stick! say my daughter.

She is not like any Chinese girl I ever saw, I say.

I brush some sand off my clothes. Sophie's clothes are dirty too, but at least she has her clothes on.

Has she done this before? ask my daughter. Has she hit you before?

She hits me all the time, Sophie say, eating ice cream.

Your family, say John.

Believe me, say my daughter.

A daughter I have, a beautiful daughter. I took care of her when she could not hold her head up. I took care of her before she could argue with me, when she was a little girl with two pigtails, one of them always crooked. I took care of her when we have to escape from China, I took care of her when suddenly we live in a country with cars everywhere, if you are not careful your little girl get run over. When my husband die, I promise him I will keep the family together, even though it was just two of us, hardly a family at all.

But now my daughter take me around to look at apartments. After all, I can cook, I can clean, there's no reason I cannot live by myself, all I need is a telephone. Of course, she is sorry. Sometimes she cry, I am the one to say everything will be okay. She say she have no choice, she doesn't want to end up divorced. I say divorce is terrible, I don't know who invented this terrible idea. Instead of live with a telephone, though, surprise, I come to live with Bess.

Imagine that. Bess make an offer and, sure enough, where she come from, people mean for you to move in when they say things like that. A crazy idea, go to live with someone else's family, but she like to have some female company, not like my daughter, who does not believe in company. These days when my daughter visit, she does not bring Sophie. Bess say we should give Nattie time, we will see Sophie again soon. But seems like my daughter have more presentation than ever before, every time she come she have to leave.

I have a family to support, she say, and her voice is heavy, as if soaking wet. I have a young daughter and a depressed husband and no one to turn to.

When she say no one to turn to, she mean me.

These days my beautiful daughter is so tired she can just sit there in a chair and fall asleep. John lost his job again, already, but still they rather hire a baby-sitter than ask me to help, even they can't afford it. Of course, the new baby-sitter is much younger, can run around. I don't know if Sophie these days is wild or not wild. She call me Meanie, but she like to kiss me too, sometimes. I remember that every time I see a child on TV. Sophie like to grab my hair, a fistful in each hand, and then kiss me smack on the nose. I never see any other child kiss that way.

The satellite TV has so many channels, more channels than I can count, including a Chinese channel from the Mainland and a Chinese channel from Taiwan, but most of the time I watch bloopers with Bess. Also, I watch the bird feeder—so many, many kinds of birds come. The Shea sons hang around all the time, asking when will I go home, but Bess tell them, Get lost.

She's a permanent resident, say Bess. She isn't going anywhere.

Then she wink at me, and switch the channel with the remote control.

Of course, I shouldn't say Irish this, Irish that, especially now I am become honorary Irish myself, according to Bess. Me! Who's Irish? I say, and she laugh. All the same, if I could mention one thing about some of the Irish, not all of them of course, I like to mention this: Their talk just stick. I don't know how Bess Shea learn to use her words, but sometimes I hear what she say a long time later. *Permanent resident. Not going anywhere.* Over and over I hear it, the voice of Bess.

BIRTHMATES

This was what responsibility meant in a dinosaur industry, toward the end of yet another quarter of bad-to-worse news: that you called the travel agent back, and even though there was indeed an economy room in the hotel where the conference was being held, a room overlooking the cooling towers, you asked if there wasn't something still cheaper. And when Marie-the-new-girl came back with something amazingly cheap, you took it—only to discover, as Art Woo was discovering now, that the doors were locked after nine o'clock. The neighborhood had looked not great but not bad, and the building itself, regular enough. Brick, four stories, a rolled-up awning. A bright-lit hotel logo, with a raised-plastic, smiling sun. But there was a kind of crossbar rigged across the inside of the glass door, and that was not at all regular. A two-by-four, it appeared, wrapped in rust-colored carpet. Above this, inside the glass, hung a small gray sign. If the taxi had not left, Art might not have rung the buzzer, as per the instructions.

But the taxi had indeed left, and the longer Art huddled on the stoop in the clumpy December snow, the emptier and more poorly lit the street appeared. His buzz was answered by an enormous black man wearing a neck brace. The shoulder seams of the man's blue waffle-weave jacket were visibly straining; around the brace was tied a necktie, which reached only a third of the way down his chest. All the same, it was neatly fastened together with a hotel-logo tie tack about two inches from the bottom. The tie tack was smiling; the man was not. He held his smooth, round face perfectly expressionless, and he lowered his gaze at every opportunity—not so that it was rude, but so that it was clear he wasn't selling anything to anybody. Regulation tie, thought Art. Regulation jacket. He wondered if the man would turn surly soon enough.

For Art had come to few conclusions about life in his forty-nine years, but this was one of them: that men turned surly when their clothes didn't fit them. This man, though, belied the rule. He was courteous, almost formal in demeanor; and if the lobby seemed not only too small for him, like his jacket, but also too much like a bus station, what with its smoked mirror wall, and its linoleum, and its fake wood, and its vending machines, what did that matter to Art? The sitting area looked as though it was in the process of being cleaned; the sixties Scandinavian chairs and couch and coffee table had been pulled every which way, as if by someone hell-bent on the dust balls. Still Art proceeded with his check-in. He was going with his gut, here as in any business situation. Here as in any business situation, he was looking foremost at the personnel, and the man with the neck brace had put him at some ease. It wasn't until after Art had taken his credit card back that he noticed, above the checkout desk, a wooden plaque from a neighborhood association. He squinted at its brass faceplate: FEWEST CUSTOMER INJURIES, 1972–73.

What about the years since '73? Had the hotel gotten more dangerous, or had other hotels gotten safer? Maybe neither. For all he knew, the neighborhood association had dissolved and was no longer distributing plaques. Art reminded himself that in life, some signs were no signs. It's what he used to tell his ex-wife, Lisa. Lisa, who loved to read everything into everything; Lisa, who was attuned. She left him on a day when she saw a tree get split by lightning. Of course, that was an extraordinary thing to see. An event of a lifetime. Lisa said the tree had sizzled. He wished he had seen it, too. But what did it mean, except that the tree had been the tallest in the neighborhood, and was no longer? It meant nothing; ditto for the plaque. Art made his decision, which perhaps was not the right decision. Perhaps he should have looked for another hotel.

But it was late—on the way out, his plane had sat on the runway, just sat and sat, as if it were never going to take off—and God only knew what he would have ended up paying if he had relied on a cabbie simply to take him somewhere else. Forget twice—it could have been three, four times what he would have paid for that room with the view of the cooling towers, easy. At this hour, after all, and that was a conference rate.

So he double-locked his door instead. He checked behind the hollow-core doors of the closet, and under the steel-frame bed, and also in the swirly-green shower stall unit. He checked behind the seascapes to be sure there weren't any peepholes. The window opened onto a fire escape; not much he could do about that except check the window locks. Big help that those were—a sure deterrent for the subset of all burglars that was burglars too skittish to break glass. Which was what percent of intruders, probably? Ten percent? Fifteen? He closed the drapes, then decided he would be more comfortable with the drapes open. He wanted to be able to see what approached, if anything did. He unplugged the handset of his phone from the base, a calculated risk. On the one hand, he wouldn't be able to call the police if there was an intruder. On the other, he would be armed. He had read somewhere a story about a woman who threw the handset of her phone at an attacker, and killed him. Needless to say, there had been some luck involved in that eventuality. Still, Art thought that

(a) surely he could throw as hard as that woman, and (b) even without the luck, his throw would most likely be hard enough to slow up an intruder at least. Especially since this was an old handset, the hefty kind that made you feel the seriousness of human communication. In a newer hotel, he probably would have had a lighter phone, with lots of buttons he would never use but which would make him feel he had many resources at his disposal. In the conference hotel, there were probably buttons for the health club, and for the concierge, and for the three restaurants, and for room service. He tried not to think about this as he went to sleep, clutching the handset.

He did not sleep well.

In the morning, he debated whether to take the handset with him into the elevator. It wasn't like a knife, say, that could be whipped out of nowhere. Even a pistol at least fit in a guy's pocket. A telephone handset did not. All the same, he took it with him. He tried to carry it casually, as if he was going out for a run and using it for a hand weight, or as if he was in the telephone business.

He strode down the hall. Victims shuffled; that's what everybody said. A lot of mugging had to do with nonverbal cues, which is why Lisa used to walk tall after dark, sending vibes. For this, he used to tease her. If she was so worried, she should lift weights and run, the way he did. That, he maintained, was the substantive way of helping oneself. She had agreed. For a while they had met after work at the gym. Then she dropped a weight on her toe and decided she preferred to sip piña coladas and watch. Naturally, he grunted on. But to what avail? Who could appreciate his pectorals through his suit and overcoat? Pectorals had no deterrent value, that was what he was thinking now. And he was, though not short, not tall. He continued striding. Sending vibes. He was definitely going to eat in the dining room of the hotel where the conference was being held, he decided. What's more, he was going to have a full American breakfast with bacon and eggs, none of this continental bullshit.

In truth, he had always considered the sight of men eating croissants slightly ridiculous, especially at the beginning, when for the first bite they had to maneuver the point of the crescent into their mouths. No matter what a person did, he ended up with an asymmetrical mouthful of pastry, which he then had to relocate with his tongue to a more central location. This made him look less purposive than he might. Also, croissants were more apt than other breakfast foods to spray little flakes all over one's clean dark suit. Art himself had accordingly never ordered a croissant in any working situation, and he believed that attention to this sort of detail was how it was that he had not lost his job like so many of his colleagues.

This was, in other words, how it happened that he was still working in a dying industry, and was now carrying a telephone handset with him into the elevator. Art braced himself as the elevator doors opened slowly, jerkily, in the low-gear manner of elevator doors in the Third World. He strode in, and was surrounded by, of all things, children. Down in the lobby, too, there were children and, here and there, women he knew to be mothers by their looks of dogged exasperation. A welfare hotel! He laughed out loud. Almost everyone was black; the white children stood out like little missed opportunities of the type that made Art's boss throw his tennis racket across the room. Of course, the racket was always in its padded protective cover and not in much danger of getting injured, though the person in whose vicinity it was aimed sometimes was. Art once suffered what he rather hoped would turn out to be a broken nose, but was only a bone bruise. There was so little skin discoloration that people had a hard time believing the incident had actually taken place. Yet it had. *Don't talk to me about fault. Bottom line, it's you Japs who are responsible for this whole fucking mess,* his boss had said. Never mind that what was the matter with minicomputers, really, was personal computers, a wholly American phenomenon. And never mind that Art could have sued over this incident if he could have proved that it had happened. Some people, most notably Lisa, thought he at least ought to have quit.

But he didn't sue and he didn't quit. He took his tennis racket on the nose, so to speak, and when his boss apologized the next day for losing control, Art said he understood. And when his boss said that Art shouldn't take what he said personally—that he knew Art was not a Jap, but a Chink, plus he had called someone else a lazy Wop that very morning, it was just his style—Art said again that he understood, and also that he hoped his boss would remember Art's great understanding come promotion time. Which his boss did, to Art's satisfaction. In Art's view, this was a victory. In Art's view, he had made a deal out of the incident. He had perceived leverage where others would only have perceived affront. He had maintained a certain perspective.

But this certain perspective was, in addition to the tree, why Lisa had left him. He thought of that now, the children underfoot, his handset in hand. So many children. It was as if he were seeing before him all the children he would never have. His heart lost muscle. A child in a red running suit ran by, almost grabbed the handset out of Art's grasp. Then another, in a brown jacket with a hood. Art looked up. A group of grade-school boys was arrayed about the seating area, watching. Art had become the object of a dare, apparently; realizing this, he felt renewed enough to want to laugh again. When a particularly small child swung by in his turn—a child of maybe five or six, small enough to be wearing snow pants—Art almost tossed the handset to him. But who wanted to be charged for a missing phone?

As it was, Art wondered if he shouldn't put the handset back in his room rather than carry it around all day. For what was he going to do at the hotel where the conference was, check it? He imagined himself running into Billy Shore—that was his counterpart at Info-Edge, and his competitor in the insurance market. A man with no management ability, and no technical background, either, but he could offer customers a personal computer option, which Art could not. What's more, Billy had been a quarterback in college. This meant he strutted around as though it still mattered that he had connected with his tight end in the final minutes of what Art could not help but think of as the Wilde-Beastie game. And it meant that Billy was sure to ask him, *What are you doing with a phone in your hand? Talking to yourself again?* Making everyone around them laugh.

Billy was that kind of guy. He had come up through sales, and was always cracking a certain type of joke—about drinking, or sex, or how much the wife shopped. Of course, he never used those words. He never called things by their plain names. He always talked in terms of *knocking back some brewskis,* or *running the triple option,* or *doing some damage.* He made assumptions as though it were a basic bodily function. Of course his knowledge was the common knowledge. Of course people understood what it was that he was referring to so delicately. *Listen, champ,* he said, putting his arm around you. If he was smug, it was in an affable kind of way. *So what do you think the poor people are doing tonight?* Billy not only spoke what Art called Mainstreamese, he spoke such a pure dialect of it that Art once asked him if he realized he was a pollster's delight. He spoke the thoughts of thousands, Art told him; he breathed their very words. Naturally, Billy did not respond, except to say, *What's that?* and turn away. He rubbed his torso as he turned, as if ruffling his chest hairs through the long-staple cotton. Primate behavior, Lisa used to call this. It was her belief that neckties evolved in order to check this very motion, uncivilized as it was. She also believed that this was the sort of thing you never saw Asian men do—at least not if they were brought up properly.

Was that true? Art wasn't so sure. Lisa had grown up on the West Coast. She was full of Asian consciousness, whereas all he knew was that no one had so much as smiled politely at his pollster remark. On the other hand, the first time Art was introduced to Billy, and Billy said, *Art Woo, how's that for a nice Pole-ack name,* everyone broke right up in great rolling guffaws. Of course, they laughed the way people laughed at conferences, which was not because something was really funny, but because it was part of being a good guy, and because they didn't want to appear to have missed their cue.

The phone, the phone. If only Art could fit it in his briefcase! But his briefcase was overstuffed; it was always overstuffed; really, it was too bad he had the slim silhouette type, and hard-side besides. Italian. That was Lisa's doing; she thought the fatter kind made him look like a salesman. Not that there was anything the matter with that, in his view. Billy Shore notwithstanding, sales were important. But she was the liberal arts type, Lisa was, the type who did not like to think about money, but only about her feelings. Money was not money to her, but support, and then a means of support much inferior to hand-holding or other forms of fingerplay. She did not believe in a modern-day economy, in which everyone played a part in a large and complex whole that introduced efficiencies that at least theoretically raised everyone's standard of living. She believed in expressing herself. Also in taking classes, and in knitting. There was nothing, she believed, like taking a walk in the autumn woods wearing a hand-knit sweater. Of course, she did look beautiful in them, especially the violet ones. That was her color—Asians are winters, she always said—and sometimes she liked to wear the smallest smidgen of matching violet eyeliner.

Little Snowpants ran at Art again, going for the knees. A tackle, thought Art as he went down. Red Running Suit snatched away the handset and went sprinting off, trimphant. Teamwork! The children chortled together. How could Art not smile, even if they had gotten his overcoat dirty? He brushed himself off, ambled over.

"Hey, guys," he said. "That was some move back there."

"Ching chong polly wolly wing wong," said Little Snowpants.

"Now, now, that's no way to talk," said Art.

"Go to hell!" said Brown Jacket, pulling at the corners of his eyes to make them slanty.

"Listen up," said Art. "I'll make you a deal." Really he only meant to get the handset back, so as to avoid getting charged for it.

But the next thing he knew, something had hit his head with a crack, and he was out.

Lisa had left in a more or less amicable way. She had not called a lawyer, or a mover. She had simply pressed his hands with both of hers and, in her most California voice, said, *Let's be nice.* Then she had asked him if he wouldn't help her move her boxes, at least the heavy ones. He had helped. He had carried the heavy boxes, and also the less heavy ones. Being a weight lifter, after all. He had sorted books and rolled glasses into pieces of newspaper, feeling all the while like a statistic. A member of the modern age, a story for their friends to rake over, and all because he had not gone with Lisa to her grieving group. Or at least that was the official beginning of the trouble. Probably the real beginning had been when Lisa—no, *they*—had trouble getting pregnant. When they decided to, as the saying went, do infertility. Or had he done the deciding, as Lisa later maintained? He had thought it was a joint decision, though it was true that he had done the analysis that led to the joint decision. He had been the one to figure the odds, to do the projections. He had drawn the decision tree according to whose branches they had nothing to lose by going ahead.

Neither one of them had realized how much would be involved—the tests, the procedures, the drugs, the ultrasounds. Lisa's arms were black and blue from having her blood drawn every day, and before long he was giving practice shots to an orange, that he might prick her some more. Then he was telling her to take a breath so that on the exhale he could poke her in the buttocks. This was nothing like poking an orange. The first time, he broke out in such a sweat that his vision blurred; he pulled the needle out slowly and crookedly, occasioning a most unorangelike cry. The second time, he wore a sweatband. Her ovaries swelled to the point where he could feel them through her jeans.

Art still had the used syringes—snapped in half and stored, as per their doctor's recommendation, in plastic soda bottles. Lisa had left him those. Bottles of medical waste, to be disposed of responsibly, meaning that he was probably stuck with them, ha-ha, for the rest of his life. This was his souvenir of their ordeal. Hers was sweeter—a little pile of knit goods. For through it all, she had knit, as if to demonstrate an alternative use of needles. Sweaters, sweaters, but also baby blankets, mostly to give away, only one or two to keep. She couldn't help herself. There was anesthesia, and egg harvesting, and anesthesia and implanting, until she finally did get pregnant, twice. The third time, she went to four and a half months before the doctors found a problem. On the amnio, it showed up, brittle-bone disease—a genetic abnormality such as could happen to anyone.

He steeled himself for another attempt; she grieved. And this was the difference between them, that he saw hope, still, some feeble, skeletal hope, where she saw loss. She called the fetus her baby, though it was not a baby, just a baby-to-be, as he tried to say; as even the grieving-group facilitator tried to say. Lisa said Art didn't understand, couldn't possibly understand. She said it was something you understood with your body, and that it was not his body, but hers, which knew the baby, loved the baby, lost the baby. In the grieving class, the women agreed. They commiserated. They bonded, subtly affirming their common biology by doing 85 percent of the talking. The room was painted mauve—a feminine color that seemed to support them in their process. At times, it seemed that the potted palms were female, too, nodding, nodding, though really their sympathy was just rising air from the heating vents. Other husbands started missing sessions—they never talked anyway, you hardly noticed their absence—and finally he missed some also. One, maybe two, for real reasons, nothing cooked up. But the truth was, as Lisa sensed, that he thought she had lost perspective. They could try again, after all. What did it help to despair? Look, they knew they could get pregnant and, what's more, sustain the pregnancy. That was progress. But she was like an island in her grief—a retreating island, if there was such a thing, receding toward the horizon of their marriage, and then to its vanishing point.

Of course, he had missed her terribly at first. Now he missed her still, but more sporadically, at odd moments—for example, now, waking up in a strange room with ice on his head. He was lying on an unmade bed just like the bed in his room, except that everywhere around it were heaps of what looked to be blankets and clothes. The only clothes on a hanger were his jacket and overcoat; these hung neatly, side by side, in the otherwise-empty closet. There was also an extra table in this room, with a two-burner hot plate, a pan on top of that, and a pile of dishes. A brown cube refrigerator. The drapes were closed. A chair had been pulled up close to him; the bedside light was on. A woman was leaning into its circle, mopping his brow.

"Don't you move, now," she said.

She was the shade of black Lisa used to call mochaccino, and she was wearing a blue flowered apron. Kind eyes; a long face— the kind of face where you could see the muscles of the jaw working alongside the cheekbone. An upper lip like an archery bow; a graying Afro, shortish. She smelled of smoke. Nothing unusual except that she was so very thin, about the thinnest person he had ever seen, and yet she was cooking something—burning something, it seemed, though maybe the smell was just a hair fallen onto the heating element. She stood up to tend the pan. The acrid smell faded. He saw powder on the table. White; there was a plastic bag full of it. His eyes widened. He sank back, trying to figure out what to do. His head pulsed. Tylenol, he needed, two. Lisa always took one because she was convinced the dosages recommended were based on large male specimens, and though she had never said that she thought he ought to keep it to one also, not being so tall, he was adamant about taking two. Two, two, two. He wanted his drugs; he wanted them now. And his own drugs, that was, not somebody else's.

"Those kids kind of rough," said the woman. "They getting to that age. I told them one of these days somebody gonna get hurt, and sure enough, they knocked you right out. You might as well been hit with a bowling ball. I never saw anything like it. We called the Man, but they got other things on their mind besides to come see about trouble here. Nobody shot, so they went on down to the Dunkin' Donuts. They know they can count on a ruckus there." She winked. "How you feelin? That egg hurt?"

He felt his head. A lump sat right on top of it, incongruous as something left by a glacier. What were those called, those stray boulders you saw perched in hair-raising positions? On cliffs? He thought.

"I feel like I died and came back to life headfirst," he said.

"I gonna make you something nice. Make you feel a whole lot better."

"Uh," said Art. "If you don't mind, I'd rather just have a Tylenol. You got any Tylenol? I had some in my briefcase. If I still have my briefcase."

"Your what?"

"My briefcase," said Art again, with a panicky feeling. "Do you know what happened to my briefcase?"

"Oh, it's right by the door. I'll get it, don't move."

Then there it was, his briefcase, its familiar hard-sided Italian slenderness resting right on his stomach. He clutched it. "Thank you," he whispered.

"You need help with that thing?"

"No," said Art. But when he opened the case, it slid, and everything spilled out—his notes, his files, his papers. All that figuring. How strange his concerns looked on this brown shag carpet.

"Here," said the woman. And again—"I'll get it, don't move"—as gently, beautifully, she gathered up all the folders and put them in the case. There was an odd, almost practiced finesse to her movements; the files could have been cards in a card dealer's hands. "I used to be a nurse," she explained, as if reading his mind. "I picked up a few folders in my time. Here's the Tylenol."

"I'll have two."

"Course you will," she said. "Two Tylenol and some hot milk with honey. Hope you don't mind the powdered. We just got moved here, we don't have no supplies. I used to be a nurse, but I don't got no milk and I don't got no Tylenol, my guests got to bring their own. How you like that."

Art laughed as much as he could. "You got honey, though. How's that?"

"I don't know, it got left here by somebody," said the nurse. "Hope there's nothing growing in it."

Art laughed again, then let her help him sit up to take his pills. The nurse—her name was Cindy—plumped his pillows. She administered his milk. Then she sat—very close to him, it seemed—and chatted amiably about this and that. How she wasn't going to be staying at the hotel for too long, how her kids had had to switch schools, how she wasn't afraid to take in a strange, injured man. After all, she grew up in the projects; she could take care of herself. She showed him her switchblade, which had somebody's initials carved on it, she didn't know whose. She had never used it, she said, somebody gave it to her. And that somebody didn't know whose initials those were, either, she said, at least so far as she knew. Then she lit a cigarette and smoked while he told her first about his conference and then about how he had ended up at this hotel by mistake. He told her the latter with some hesitation, hoping he wasn't offending her. She laughed with a cough, emitting a series of smoke puffs.

"Sure musta been a shock," she said. "End up in a place like this. This ain't no place for a nice boy like you."

That stung a little, being called *boy*. But more than the stinging, he felt something else. "What about you? It's no place for you, either, you and your kids."

"Maybe so," she said. "But that's how the Almighty planned it, right? You folk rise up while we set and watch." She said this with so little rancor, with something so like intimacy, that it almost seemed an invitation of sorts.

Maybe he was kidding himself. Maybe he was assuming things, just like Billy Shore, just like men throughout the ages. Projecting desire where there was none, assigning and imagining, and in juicy detail. Being Asian didn't exempt him from that. *You folk.*

Art was late, but it didn't much matter. His conference was being held in conjunction with a much larger conference, the real draw; the idea being that maybe between workshops and on breaks, the conferees would drift down and see what minicomputers could do for them. That mostly meant lunch, which probably would be slow at best. In the meantime, things were totally dead, allowing Art to appreciate just how much the trade-show floor had shrunk—down to a fraction of what it had been in previous years, and the booths were not what they had been, either. It used to be that the floor was crammed with the fanciest booths on the market. Art's was twenty by twenty; it took days to put together. Now you saw blank spots on the floor where exhibitors didn't even bother to show up, and those weren't even as demoralizing as some of the makeshift jobbies—exhibit booths that looked like high school science-fair projects. They might as well have been made out of cardboard and Magic Marker. Art himself had a booth you could buy from an airplane catalog, the kind that rolled up into Cordura bags. And people were stingy with brochures now, too. Gone were the twelve-page, four-color affairs. Now the pamphlets were four-page, two-color, with extrabold graphics for attempted pizzazz, and not everybody got one, only people who were serious.

Art set up. Then, even though he should have been manning his spot, he drifted from booth to booth, saying hello to people he should have seen at breakfast. They were happy to see him, to talk shop, to pop some grapes off the old grapevine. Really, if he hadn't been staying in a welfare hotel, he would have felt downright respected. *You folk.* What folk did Cindy mean? Maybe she was just being matter-of-fact, keeping her perspective. Although how could anyone be so matter-of-fact about something so bitter? He wondered this even as he imagined taking liberties with her. These began with a knock on her door and coursed through some hot times but finished (what a good boy he was) with him rescuing her and her children (he wondered how many there were) from their dead-end life. What was the matter with him, that he could not imagine mating without legal sanction? His libido was not what it should be, clearly, or at least it was not what Billy Shore's was. Art tried to think *game plan,* but in truth he could not even identify what a triple option would be in this case. All he knew was that, assuming, to begin with, that she was willing, he couldn't sleep with a woman like Cindy and then leave her flat. She could *you folk* him, he could never *us folk* her.

He played with some software at a neighboring booth. It appeared interesting enough but kept crashing, so he couldn't tell much. Then he dutifully returned to his own booth, where he was visited by a number of people he knew, people with whom he was friendly—the sort of people to whom he might have shown pictures of his children. He considered telling one or two of them about the events of the morning. Not about the invitation that might not have been an invitation, but about finding himself in a welfare hotel and being beaned with his own telephone. Phrases drifted through his head. *Not as bad as you'd think. You'd be surprised how friendly. And how unpretentious. Though, of course, no health club.* But in the end, the subject simply did not come up and did not come up, until he realized that he was keeping it to himself, and that he was committing more resources to this task than he had readily available. He felt invaded—as if he had been infected by a self-replicating bug. Something that was iterating and iterating, crowding the cpu. The secret was intolerable; it was bound to spill out of him sooner or later. He just hoped it wouldn't be sooner.

He just hoped it wouldn't be to Billy Shore, for whom Art had begun to search, so as to be certain to avoid him.

Art had asked about Billy at the various booths, but no one had seen him; his absence spooked Art. When finally some real live conferees stopped by to see his wares, Art had trouble concentrating. Everywhere in the conversation he was missing opportunities, he knew it. And all because his cpu was full of iterating nonsense. Not too long ago, in looking over some database software in which were loaded certain fun facts about people in the industry, Art had looked up Billy, and discovered that he had been born the same day Art was, only four years later. It just figured that Billy would be younger. That was irritating. But Art was happy for the information, too. He had made a note of it, so that when he ran into Billy at this conference, he could kid him about their birthdays. Now, he rehearsed. *Have I got a surprise for you. I always knew you were a Leo. I believe this makes us birthmates.* Anything not to mention the welfare hotel and all that had happened there.

In the end, Art did not run into Billy at all. In the end, Art wondered about Billy all day, only to learn, finally, that Billy had moved on to a new job in the Valley, with a start-up. In personal computers, naturally. A good move, no matter what kind of beating he took on his house.

"Life is about the long term," said Ernie Ford, the informant. "And let's face it, there is no long term here."

Art agreed as warmly as he could. In one way, he was delighted that his competitor had left. If nothing else, that would mean a certain amount of disarray at Info-Edge, which was good news for Art. The insurance market was, unfortunately, some 40 percent of his business, and he could use any advantage he could get. Another bonus was that Art was never going to have to see Billy again. Billy his birthmate, with his jokes and his Mainstreamese. Still, Art felt depressed.

"We should all have gotten out way before this," he said.

"Truer words were never spoke," said Ernie. Ernie had never been a particular friend of Art's, but talking about Billy was somehow making him chummier. "I'd have packed my bags by now if it weren't for the wife, the kids—they don't want to leave their friends, you know? Plus, the oldest is a junior in high school. We can't afford for him to move now. He's got to stay put and make those nice grades so he can make a nice college. That means I've got to stay, if it means pushing McMuffins for Ronald McDonald. But now you . . ."

"Maybe I should go," said Art.

"Definitely, you should go," said Ernie. "What's keeping you?"

"Nothing," said Art. "I'm divorced now. And that's that, right? Sometimes people get undivorced, but you can't exactly count on it."

"Go," said Ernie. "Take my advice. If I hear of anything, I'll send it your way."

"Thanks," said Art.

But of course he did not expect that Ernie would likely turn anything up soon. It had been a long time since anyone had called Art or anybody else he knew of. Too many people had gotten stranded, and they were too desperate, everybody knew it. Also, the survivors were looked upon with suspicion. Anybody who was any good had jumped ship early, that was the conventional wisdom. There was Art, struggling to hold on to his job, only to discover that there were times you didn't want to hold on to your job—times you ought to maneuver for the golden parachute and jump. Times the goal was to get yourself fired. Who would have figured that?

A few warm-blooded conferees at the end of the day—at least they were polite. Then, as he was packing up to return to the hotel, a surprise. A headhunter approached him, a friend of Ernest's, he said.

"Ernest?" said Art. "Oh, Ernie! Ford! Of course!"

The headhunter was a round, ruddy man with a ring of hair like St. Francis of Assisi, and, sure enough, a handful of bread crumbs. A great opportunity, he said. Right now he had to run, but he knew just the guy Art had to meet, a guy who was coming in that evening. For something else, it happened, but he also needed someone like Art. Needed him yesterday, really. Should've been a priority. Might just be a match. Maybe a quick breakfast in the a.m.? Could he call in an hour or so? Art said, Of course. And when Saint Francis asked his room number, Art hesitated, but then gave the name of the welfare hotel. How would Saint Francis know what kind of hotel it was? Art gave the name out confidently, making his manner count. He almost hadn't made it to the conference at all, he said. Being so busy. It was only at the last minute that he realized he could do it. Things moved around, he found an opening and figured what the hell. But it was too late to book the conference hotel. Hence he was staying elsewhere.

Success. All day Art's mind had been churning; suddenly it seemed to empty. He might as well have been Billy, born on the same day as Art was, but in another year, under different stars. How much simpler things seemed. He did not labor on two, three, six tasks at once, multiprocessing. He knew one thing at a time, and that thing just now was that the day was a victory. He walked briskly back to the hotel. He crossed the lobby in a no-nonsense manner. An impervious man. He did not knock on Cindy's door. He was moving on, moving west. There would be a good job there, and a new life. Perhaps he would take up tennis. Perhaps he would own a Jacuzzi. Perhaps he would learn to like all those peculiar foods people ate out there, like jicama, and seaweed. Perhaps he would go macrobiotic.

It wasn't until he got to his room that he remembered that his telephone had no handset.

He sat on his bed. There was a noise at his window, followed, sure enough, by someone's shadow. He wasn't even surprised.

Anyway, the fellow wasn't stopping at Art's room, at least not on this trip. That was luck. *You folk,* Cindy had said, taking back the ice bag. Art could see her perspective; he was luckier than she, by far. But just now, as the shadow crossed his window again, he thought mostly about how unarmed he was. If he had a telephone, he would probably call Lisa—that was how big a pool seemed to be forming around him, all of a sudden; an ocean, it seemed. Also, he would call the police. But first he would call Lisa, and see how she felt about his possibly moving west. *Quite possibly,* he would say, not wanting to make it sound as though he was calling her for nothing—not wanting to make it sound as though he was awash, at sea, perhaps drowning. He would not want to sound like a haunted man; he would not want to sound as though he was calling from a welfare hotel, years too late, to say *Yes, that was a baby we had together, it would have been a baby.* For he could not help now but recall the doctor explaining about that child, a boy, who had appeared so mysteriously perfect in the ultrasound. Transparent, he had looked, and gelatinous, all soft head and quick heart; but he would have, in being born, broken every bone in his body.

THE WATER
FAUCET VISION

To protect my sister, Mona, and me from the pains—or, as they pronounced it, the *pens*—of life, my parents did their fighting in Shanghai dialect, which we didn't understand; and when my father one day pitched a brass vase through the kitchen window, my mother told us he had done it by accident.

"By accident?" said Mona.

My mother chopped the foot off a mushroom.

"By accident?" said Mona. "By *accident?*"

Later, I tried to explain to her that she shouldn't have persisted like that, but it was hopeless.

"What's the matter with throwing things?" she shrugged. "He was *mad.*"

That was the difference between Mona and me: fighting was just fighting to her. If she worried about anything, it was only that she might turn out too short to become a ballerina, in which case she was going to be a piano player.

I, on the other hand, was going to be a martyr. I was in fifth grade then, and the hyperimaginative sort—the kind of girl who grows morbid in Catholic school, who longs to be chopped or frozen to death but then has nightmares about it from which she wakes up screaming and clutching a stuffed bear. It was not a bear that I clutched, though, but a string of three malachite beads that I had found in the marsh by the old aqueduct one day. Apparently once part of a necklace, they were each wonderfully striated and swirled, and slightly humped toward the center, like a jelly-fish; so that if I squeezed one, it would slip smoothly away, with a grace that altogether enthralled and—on those dream-harrowed nights—soothed me, soothed me as nothing had before or has since. Not that I've lacked occasion for soothing: Though it's been four months since my mother died, there are still nights when sleep stands away from me, stiff as a well-paid sentry. But that is another story. Back then, I had my malachite beads, and if I worried them long and patiently enough, I was sure to start feeling better, more awake, even a little special—imagining, as I liked to, that my nightmares were communications from the Almighty Himself, preparation for my painful destiny. Discussing them with Patty Creamer, who had also promised her life to God, I called them "almost visions"; and Patty, her mouth wadded with the three or four sticks of Doublemint she always seemed to have going at once, said, "I bet you'll be doin' miracleth by seventh grade."

Miracles. Today Patty laughs to think she ever spent good time stewing on such matters, her attention having long turned to rugs, and artwork, and antique Japanese bureaus—things she believes in.

"A good bureau's more than just a bureau," she explained last time we had lunch. "It's a hedge against life. I tell you, if there's one thing I believe, it's that cheap stuff's just money out the window. Nice stuff, on the other hand—now *that* you can always cash out, if life gets rough. *That* you can count on."

In fifth grade, though, she counted on different things.

"You'll be doing miracles, too," I told her, but she shook her shaggy head and looked doleful.

"Na' me," she chomped. "Buzzit's okay. The kin' things I like, prayers work okay on."

"Like?"

"Like you 'member that dreth I liked?"

She meant the yellow one, with the crisscross straps.

"Well gueth what."

"Your mom got it for you."

She smiled. "And I only jutht prayed for it for a week," she said.

As for myself, though, I definitely wanted to be able to perform a wonder or two. Miracle working! It was the carrot of carrots. It kept me doing my homework, taking the sacraments; it kept me mournfully on key in music hour, while my classmates hiccuped and squealed their carefree hearts away. Yet I couldn't have said what I wanted such powers for, exactly. That is, I thought of them the way one might think of, say, an ornamental sword—as a kind of collectible, which also happened to be a means of defense.

But then Patty's father walked out on her mother, and for the first time, there was a miracle I wanted to do. I wanted it so much, I could see it: Mr. Creamer made into a spitball. Mr. Creamer shot through a straw into the sky. Mr. Creamer unrolled and replumped, plop back on Patty's doorstep. I would've cleaned out his mind and given him a shave en route. I would've given him a box of peanut fudge, tied up with a ribbon, to present to Patty with a kiss.

But instead, all I could do was try to tell her he'd come back.

"He will not, he will not!" she sobbed. "He went on a boat to Rio Deniro. To Rio Deniro!"

I tried to offer her a stick of gum, but she wouldn't take it.

"He said he would rather look at water than at my mom's fat face. He said he would rather look at water than at me." Now she was really wailing, and holding her ribs so tightly that she almost seemed to be hurting herself—so tightly that just looking at her arms wound around her like snakes made my heart feel squeezed.

I patted her on the arm. A one-winged pigeon waddled by.

"He said I wasn't even his kid, he said I came from Uncle Johnny. He said I was garbage, just like my mom and Uncle Johnny. He said I wasn't even his kid, he said I wasn't his Patty, he said I came from Uncle Johnny!"

"From your Uncle Johnny?" I said stupidly.

"From Uncle Johnny," she cried. "From Uncle Johnny!"

"He said that?"

She kept crying.

I tried again. "Oh Patty, don't cry," I said. Then I said, "Your dad was a jerk anyway."

The pigeon produced a large runny dropping.

It was a good twenty minutes before Patty was calm enough for me to run to the girls' room to get her some toilet paper; and by the time I came back she was sobbing again, saying "to Rio Deniro, to Rio Deniro" over and over, as though the words had stuck in her and couldn't be gotten out. Seeing as how we had missed the regular bus home and the late bus, too, I had to leave her a second time to go call my mother, who was only mad until she heard what had happened. Then she came and picked us up, and bought us each a Fudgsicle.

Some days later, Patty and I started a program to work on getting her father home. It was a serious business. We said extra prayers, and lit votive candles. I tied my malachite beads to my uniform belt, fondling them as though they were a rosary, and I a nun. We even took to walking about the school halls with our hands folded—a sight so ludicrous that our wheeze of a principal personally took us aside one day.

"I must tell you," she said, using her nose as a speaking tube, "that there is really no need for such peee-ity."

But we persisted, promising to marry God and praying to

every saint we could think of. We gave up gum, then gum and Slim Jims both, then gum and Slim Jims and ice cream; and when even that didn't work, we started on more innovative things. The first was looking at flowers. We held our hands beside our eyes like blinders as we hurried past the violets by the flagpole. Next it was looking at boys: Patty gave up angel-eyed Jamie Halloran, and I, gymnastic Anthony Rossi. It was hard, but in the end our efforts paid off. Mr. Creamer came back a month later, and though he brought with him nothing but dysentery, he was at least too sick to have all that much to say.

Then, in the course of a fight with my father, my mother somehow fell out of their bedroom window.

Recently—thinking a mountain vacation might cheer me—I sublet my apartment to a handsome but somber newlywed couple, who turned out to be every bit as responsible as I'd hoped. They cleaned out even the eggshell chips I'd sprinkled around the base of my plants as fertilizer, leaving behind only a shiny silver-plate cake server and a list of their hopes and goals for the summer. The list, tacked precariously to the back of the kitchen door, began with a fervent appeal to God to help them get their wedding thank-yous written in three weeks or less. (You could see they had originally written "two weeks" but scratched it out—no miracles being demanded here.) It went on:

> *Please help us, Almighty Father in Heaven Above, to get Ann a teaching job within a half-hour drive of here in a nice neighborhood.*
> *Please help us, Almighty Father in Heaven Above, to get John a job doing anything where he won't strain his back and that is within a half-hour drive of here.*

Please help us, Almighty Father in Heaven Above, to get us a car.

Please help us, A. F. in H. A., to learn French.

Please help us, A. F. in H. A., to find seven dinner recipes that cost less than 60 cents a serving and can be made in a half hour. And that don't have tomatoes, since You in Your Heavenly Wisdom made John allergic.

Please help us, A. F. in H. A., to avoid books in this apartment such as You in Your Heavenly Wisdom allowed John, for Your Heavenly Reasons, to find three nights ago (June 2nd).

Et cetera. In the left-hand margin they had kept score of how they had fared with their requests, and it was heartening to see that nearly all of them were marked "Yes! Praise the Lord" (sometimes shortened to "PTL"), with the sole exception of learning French, which was mysteriously marked "No! PTL to the Highest."

That note touched me. Strange and familiar both, it seemed as though it had been written by some cousin of mine—some cousin who had stayed home to grow up, say, while I went abroad and learned painful things. This, of course, is just a manner of speaking. In fact, I did my growing up at home, like anybody else.

But the learning was painful. I never knew exactly how it happened that my mother went hurtling through the air that night years ago, only that the wind had been chopping at the house, and that the argument had started about the state of the roof. Someone had been up to fix it the year before, but it wasn't a roofer, only a man my father had insisted could do just as good a job for a quarter of the price. And maybe he could have, had he not somehow managed to step through a knot in the wood under the shingles and break his uninsured ankle. Now the shingles were coming loose again, and the attic insulation was mildewing besides, and my father was wanting to sell the house altogether, which he said my mother had wanted to buy so she could send pictures of it home to her family in China.

"The Americans have a saying," he said. "They saying, 'You have to keep up with Jones family.' I'm saying if Jones family in Shanghai, you can send any picture you want, *an-y* picture. Go take picture of those rich guys' house. You want to act like rich guys, right? Go take picture of those rich guys' house."

At that point, my mother sent Mona and me to wash up, and started speaking Shanghainese. They argued for some time in the kitchen, while we listened from the top of the stairs, our faces wedged between the bumpy Spanish scrolls of the wrought-iron railing. First my mother ranted, then my father, and then they both ranted at once, until finally there was a thump, followed by a long quiet.

"Do you think they're kissing now?" said Mona. "I bet they're kissing, like this." She pursed her lips like a fish, and was about to put them to the railing when we heard my mother locking the back door. We hightailed it into bed; my parents creaked up the stairs. Everything at that point seemed fine. Once in their bedroom, though, they started up again, first softly, then more and more loudly, until my mother turned on a radio to try to disguise the noise. A door slammed; they began shouting at each other; another door slammed; a shoe or something banged the wall behind Mona's bed.

"How're we supposed to *sleep*?" said Mona, sitting up.

There was another thud; more yelling in Shanghainese; and then my mother's voice pierced the wall, in English. "So what you want I should do? Go to work like Theresa Lee?"

My father rumbled something back.

"You think you are big shot, but you never get promotion, you never get raise. All I do is spend money, right? So what do you do, you tell me. So what do you do!"

Something hit the floor so hard, our room shook.

"So kill me," screamed my mother. "You know what you are? You are failure. Failure! You are failure!"

Then there was a sudden, terrific, bursting crash—and after it, as if on a bungled cue, the serene blare of an a capella soprano picking her way down a scale.

By the time Mona and I knew to look out the window, a neighbor's pet beagle was already on the scene, sniffing and barking at my mother's body, his tail crazy with excitement. Then he was barking at my stunned and trembling father, at the shrieking ambulance, at the police, at crying Mona in her bunny-footed pajamas, and at me, barefoot in the cold grass, squeezing my sister's shoulder with one hand and clutching my malachite beads with the other.

My mother wasn't dead, only unconscious—the paramedics figured that out right away—but there was blood everywhere, and though they were reassuring about her head wounds as they strapped her to the stretcher—commenting also on how small she was, how delicate, how light—my father kept saying, *I killed her, I killed her* as the ambulance screeched and screeched headlong, forever, to the hospital. I was afraid to touch her, and glad of the metal rail between us, even though its sturdiness made her seem even frailer than she was. I wished she were bigger, somehow, and noticed, with a pang, that the new red slippers we had given her for Mother's Day had been lost somewhere along the way. How much she seemed to be leaving behind, as we careened along— still not there, still not there—Mona and Dad and the medic and I taking up the whole ambulance, all the room, so that there was no room for anything else; no room even for my mother's real self, the one who should have been pinching the color back to my father's gray face, the one who should have been calming Mona's cowlick—the one who should have been bending over us, to help us be strong, to help us get through, even as we bent over her.

Then suddenly we were there, the glowing square of the emergency room entrance opening like the gates of heaven; and immediately the talk of miracles began. Alive, a miracle. No bones broken, a miracle. A miracle that the hemlocks had cushioned her fall, a miracle that they hadn't been trimmed in a year and a half. It was a miracle that all that blood, the blood that had seemed that night to be everywhere, was from one shard of glass, a single shard, can you imagine, and as for the gash in her head, the scar would be covered by hair. The next day, my mother cheerfully described just how she would part it so that nothing would show at all.

"You're a lucky duck-duck," agreed Mona, helping herself, with a little pirouette, to the cherry atop my mother's chocolate pudding.

That wasn't enough for me, though. I was relieved, yes, but what I wanted by then was a real miracle. Not for my mother simply to have survived, but for the whole thing never to have happened—for my mother's head never to have been shaved and bandaged like that, for her high, proud forehead never to have been swollen down over her eyes, for her face and neck and hands never to have been painted so many shades of blue-black, and violet, and chartreuse. I still want those things—for my parents not to have had to live with this affair like a prickle bush between them, for my father to have been able to look my mother in her swollen eyes and curse the madman, the monster who had dared do this to the woman he loved. I wanted to be able to touch my mother without shuddering, to be able to console my father, to be able to get that crash out of my head, the sound of that soprano—so many things that I didn't know how to pray for them, that I wouldn't have known where to start even if I had had the power to work miracles, right there, right then.

A week later, when my mother's head was beginning to bristle with new hairs, I lost my malachite beads. I had been carrying them in a white cloth pouch that Patty had given me, and was swinging the pouch on my pinkie on my way home from school, when I swung just a bit too hard; the pouch went sailing in a long arc through the air, *whooshing* like a perfectly thrown basketball through one of the holes of a nearby sewer. There was no chance of fishing it out. I looked and looked, crouching on the sticky pavement until the asphalt had crazed the skin of my hands and knees, but all I could discern was an evil-smelling murk, glassy and smug and impenetrable.

My loss didn't quite hit me until I was home, but then it produced an agony all out of proportion to my string of pretty beads. I hadn't cried at all during my mother's accident, but now I was crying all afternoon, all through dinner, and then after dinner, too—crying past the point where I knew what I was crying for, wishing dimly that I had my beads to hold, wishing dimly that I could pray, but refusing, refusing, I didn't know why, until I finally fell into an exhausted sleep on the couch. There my parents left me for the night—glad, no doubt, that one of the more tedious of my childhood crises seemed to be winding off the reel of life, onto the reel of memory. They covered me, and somehow grew a pillow under my head, and, with uncharacteristic disregard for the living room rug, left some milk and Pecan Sandies on the coffee table, in case I woke up hungry. Their thoughtfulness was prescient. I did wake up in the early part of the night; and it was then, amid the unfamiliar sounds and shadows of the living room, that I had what I was sure was a true vision.

Even now, what I saw retains an odd clarity: the requisite strange light flooding the room, first orange, and then a bright yellow-green. A crackling bright burst like a Roman candle going off near the piano. There was a distinct smell of coffee, and a long silence. The room seemed to be getting colder. Nothing. A creak; the light starting to wane, then waxing again, brilliant pink now. Still nothing. Then, as the pink started to go a little purple, a perfectly normal, middle-aged man's voice, speaking something very like pig latin, told me not to despair, not to despair, my beads would be returned to me.

That was all. I sat a moment in the dark, then turned on the light, gobbled down the cookies—and in a happy flash understood that I was so good, really, so near to being a saint that my malachite beads would come back through the town water system. All I had to do was turn on all the faucets in the house. This I did, stealing quietly into the bathroom and kitchen and basement. The old spigot by the washing machine was too gunked up to be coaxed very far open, but that didn't matter. The water didn't have to be full blast, I understood that. Then I gathered together my pillow and blanket and trundled up to my bed to sleep.

By the time I woke in the morning, I knew that my beads hadn't shown up; but when I knew it for certain, I was still disappointed. And as if that weren't enough, I had to face my parents and sister, who were all abuzz with the mystery of the faucets. Not knowing what else to do, I, like a puddlebrain, told them the truth. The results were predictably painful.

"Callie had a *vision*," Mona told everyone at the bus stop. "A vision with lights, and sinks in it!"

Sinks, visions. I got it all day, from my parents, from my classmates, even from some sixth and seventh graders. Someone drew a cartoon of me with a halo over my head in one of the girls' room stalls; Anthony Rossi made gurgling noises as he walked on his hands at recess. Only Patty tried not to laugh, though even she was something less than unalloyed understanding.

"I don' think miracles are thupposed to happen in *thewers*," she said.

Such was the end of my saintly ambitions. It wasn't the end of all holiness. The ideas of purity and goodness still tippled my brain, and over the years I came slowly to grasp of what grit true faith is made. Last night, though, when my father called to say that he couldn't go on living in our old house, that he was going to move to a smaller place, another place, maybe a condo—he didn't know how, or where—I found myself still wistful for the time religion seemed all I wanted it to be. Back then, the world was a place that could be set right. One had only to direct the hand of the Almighty and say, Just here, Lord, we hurt here—and here, and here, and here.

DUNCAN IN CHINA

Duncan Hsu, foreign expert. That was his name in China. In America, it had been Duncan Hsu, dropout. He had dropped out of a military academy, a law school, a computer-programming night class, a ten-year-old soap opera of a relationship, and even, recently, out of a career-exploration minicourse. As a result, he was now thirty-seven, with many people not speaking to him—for example, his mother and, so far as he could tell, his father. His father was a master of the art of speechifying without speaking, unlike Duncan's mother, who called every day, lest Duncan forget she was not speaking to him. She called lest he imagine he had become the sort of son about whom she could boast, or lest he overlook how well his brother Arnie was doing. Arnie had started an import-export business, which now employed sixteen lucky people. Arnie drove a BMW convertible and wore wraparound sunglasses. Arnie had his car washed inside and out while he went shopping with his girlfriend from Hong Kong. Arnie was at one with the Chinese bourgeois experience.

Duncan, on the other hand, tortured himself with the idea that there had to be more to his heritage. He went to China because, having seen Sung dynasty porcelains in museums, he wanted to know more about that China—the China of the scholar-officials, the China of ineffable nobility and restraint. Duncan was no artist—art school was the one kind of school he

.ght to drop out of. But those porcelains could
/, what with their grace and purity, and delicate
.s; what with their wholeness and confidence and
 .ntortured air. They made him feel what life could be,
and wi.. his life was. They were uplifting; they were depress-
ing. That was beauty for you. Duncan had not been an Asian
anything major, but in his frequent periods of incipient employ-
ment, he had read about the tremendous integrity of the Sung
scholar-officials, and had speculated that some of their noble
code had survived in the spirit of the Long March. Should there
not be, somewhere, an iota of it left still? Maybe even in his own
family? He had had scholars in his family, after all; they had
not always been attitudinal geniuses of his brother's ilk. Some of
them had run schools. One of his father's brothers had been a
kind of horticulturist-folklorist-herbalist; he married a violinist-
entomologist. Their son, Duncan's cousin, was still alive and living in China. Perhaps Duncan would have a chance to meet him.

Or perhaps Duncan would fall in love. Later, Duncan would
remember that even before he left the United States, even before
he met the perhaps beautiful, perhaps noble, completely madden-
ing Louise, he had considered the possibility of love. For wasn't
that what happened to people in foreign lands? He'd learned that
from the movies. Anything was possible. So argued one voice in
his head, even as another said, Folly.

Folly. Almost as soon as Duncan reached Shandong, he knew that
he had come for naught, that the China of the early 1980s had
more to do with eating melon seeds around a coal heater the size
of a bread box than about Sung dynasty porcelain. He gave up his
goal easily, more easily than he would have thought possible. He
flowed, a man without dismay, and all on account of the cold. At
home he had railed against degree programs, movies, voting pro-

cedures, sports equipment. He had reviled the local Motor Vehicle Department; he had denounced mindlessness, fecklessness, spinelessness. But in China so many things were poorly run and poorly designed that there was no point in railing against them. And who could fault the people for a certain scrappy element? Certainly not in the winter. Duncan had read tableloads of books about China before he left, but none had prepared him for the plunge in mental functioning that he experienced; it was as if his thought-bearing fluids had gone viscous. There were two kinds of rooms for him now—barely heated, and unheated. There were two kinds of days—slightly warmer, and no warmer. When Duncan had a chance to catch a reflection of himself, he was amazed to see how much less baby-faced he looked here than he had at home. His face was no gaunter, and still featured dimples, but it was chapped and reddened in a cowboy-on-the-prairie kind of way, rather than smooth and shiny enough to be featured in a soap ad. This brought him a certain, specific contentment. More generally, though, he was contented when he was warm enough, and discontented when he was not. Whereas at home he had been impatient with people who thought of nothing but their comfort, now he thought of nothing but his comfort.

Already, in short, Duncan was becoming like Professor Mo, the head of the English-language program at the coal mining institute to which Duncan was assigned. Professor Mo always made sure that Duncan the foreign expert was seated next to whatever meager heat source might be available, if only so that he, as protector and guide of the foreign expert, might also sit next to the meager heat source.

"I'll order up some beer for you," he would say when he himself was thirsty. Or else, "The shark's fin soup in this restaurant's said to be marvelous. Shall I order some up?" And his arm would be in the air before Duncan had a chance to say he was allergic.

Professor Mo was a haggard man in his fifties, who walked

with one hand swinging around him as if he were practicing a one-armed breaststroke, or as if he were clearing a path through the riffraff for his personage. Once upon a time, in his idealistic youth, he had forsworn his inheritance, hoping to join the revolution. Was that not noble? And yet during the Cultural Revolution, he had been struggled against just the same. Since then, he had been reinstituted as a valued member of society because he spoke English. Now he laughed a shrill laugh. Had the Red Guards beaten him and tarred him and urinated on him? Had they incarcerated him and forced his family to abandon him? Thanks to the restoration of a fraction of his family's fortune, he inhabited one of the largest apartments in town these days; and it was his distinct pleasure to give grades to former Red Guards. Moreover, at a time when other professors were still wearing Mao jackets, Mo let his heavy quilt coat fall open so that everyone might glimpse the seedy doublebreasted suits he wore underneath. These were apparently relics of his years of study abroad—the years during which he had also picked up his strangely inflected English, along with an amazing variety of mannerisms that served to obfuscate any real sense of his being. A habit of draping one arm over the back of his chair, for example, in an exaggerated, man-of-the-world pose. A loop-de-loop manner of talking with his hands, and a way of letting his cigarette dangle so loosely from his lips that it resembled a sort of burning dribble.

"You must assign more homework," he told Duncan one day, his cigarette hanging so precipitously that Duncan worried it would fall into his lap. "Otherwise, the students will loaf about and make trouble."

"I assign four hours a day," ventured Duncan. "Where they're in class from nine o'clock to four, that seems like it ought to be enough."

"Not enough," said Professor Mo. "And no more songs. You are not engaged in a popularity contest."

"But they like songs," Duncan protested. "They specifically asked for songs." Duncan recalled the day that the class monitor, William—the students had all chosen English names for the year—had made the request on behalf of his classmates. William was a square-headed, square-bodied man, so strong that he had dug himself out from under a building after the earthquake in Tangshan. Yet in presenting the class request to Duncan, he had blushed red as a pomegranate, feeling the difficulty of his task.

"You are not engaged in a popularity contest," repeated Professor Mo.

Duncan knew what the real problem was. The real problem was that Mo, endeavoring to do as little work as possible, had elected, as his semester offering, to give a practice session every day from four to five. Whereas before Duncan arrived, Mo could count on a full class for whatever he taught, however, now he was finding that few students bothered to come. The students complained that it was a waste of time, and one had only to peek in the door, and behold Mo pontificating at the front of the room, to understand why. To begin with, though the classroom was of average size, Mo had a microphone on his desk. This was hooked up to two speakers, each on a desk of its own, flanking him. Mo took long drags of his cigarette, his chin jutting up into the air, then swooped down importantly into the mike. "Well," he drawled. "That's a matter of opinion." Pause. "One might say." The students—there were three of them—looked bored. Mo's classroom, like Duncan's, had been outfitted with an elaborate system of overhead wires, from which brown extension cords hung down, one beside each desk, so that the students could plug in their all-important tape recorders. Duncan's own class was punctuated by the constant sound of cassette tapes running out and being flipped; at times he had wondered if there was anything the students, in their avidity, would not tape. Now he had his answer. None of the students was operating his machine.

Bearing all this in mind, Duncan endeavored to deal with his supervisor in a diplomatic and sagacious manner, such as befit a foreign expert.

"Perhaps you could take over the song instruction," he suggested, though he doubted that Professor Mo could sing. "We could coordinate other parts of the curriculum, as well. I could assign the practice session as part of their homework. Make it required." Duncan tried to broach these ideas as delicately as he could.

"What a nice idea," said Mo in reply. "How very kind of you." Then he laughed, showing his nicotine-stained teeth. He looped his arm over the back of his chair with an elaborate motion related to his one-armed breaststroke—the one-armed butterfly, thought Duncan—as, with some ceremony, he recrossed his legs.

Thus did the enmity begin. Over the next few weeks, Mo did not make a comment to Duncan that did not include the word "kind." If you would be so *kind*, he said. Just a *kindly* reminder. How very *kind* of you.

The curriculum coordination Duncan had proposed did not take place, though Mo did sit in on several of Duncan's classes, presumably to make sure Duncan wasn't teaching any songs. Mo set up camp in the back of the room, drinking tea and smoking cigarettes. He read the newspaper, turning the pages so loudly that the students complained he was ruining their tapes.

"The students feel he is, well, a bit strange," allowed William one afternoon, after relaying to Duncan what he called the "difficulty."

"Like Jiang Qing, only man," said another student. The reference was to Mao's widow, an effigy of whom Duncan had recently seen, with a noose around her neck, in a park. As for the speaker, that, of course, was Louise—Louise, who from the first day had seemed to burst from the dingy rows of the classroom like a streak of pure color. Duncan had noticed that she changed her hairstyle almost every day. Yet she did not seem vain, perhaps because she was not a beautiful woman. She was, rather, inexplicably beautiful, a woman whose pedestrian features—dark eyes, a long nose, a mischievously pursed mouth—were eclipsed by the extraordinary radiance of her face.

"Seems like Professor Mo would like Gang of Four to be Gang of Five," she said.

William laughed but then looked away pointedly; so that when Duncan asked if Louise had seen the park effigy, she answered, blushing deeply, "I see nothing."

"Of course," said Duncan tactfully. "Excuse me."

It took three days for Duncan to "raise his opinion," as his students would say. But finally he said, "If you would *kindly* desist from reading the newspaper in my class, I would appreciate it."

He braced for Mo's reaction. But to his surprise, Mo smiled with a kind of satisfaction, tapped some ashes on the floor, and said, "I guessed from the start you had something inside your coat."

"What do you mean?"

"What an interesting question." Mo rehung his cigarette in his mouth. "A Chinese man, you know, would go home, figure out what my meaning is."

"I see," said Duncan, though he did not see.

"Are you Chinese?"

"Yes," said Duncan. "I mean, I don't know. I guess no." He felt, for the first time since he had come to China, too hot.

"In that case, I explain to you."

Duncan watched the ash flare. He studied his superior's hands, which were nicotine-stained, but also surprisingly delicate and fine—the hands of a ceramist. "My meaning is, I guessed from the start you are inside here"—Mo indicated the inside of his lapel—"a sarcastic brute."

"Ah," said Duncan.

"Do you understand me now?"

"Yes and no," said Duncan.

Mo smoked.

Finally, finally it was getting to be spring. That meant, first of all, that instead of winter cabbage, day in and day out, now there were other vegetables to eat—first big scallions, then spinach and leeks, then small scallions. The trees began to green, beginning with the willows, bringing shade. Quilts were hung out to air. Students went for walks. Often Duncan would glimpse Louise's small, slim figure out with one classmate or another; she seemed to pick a different classmate every day. People began to play basketball on the packed dirt court outside Duncan's window. As often as he could, Duncan joined them. This brought him real pleasure, especially the couple of times Louise managed to goad some of the other women into playing with the guys. How startlingly quick and savvy she was! Agile as a greyhound, she was able to find her merry way around players far bigger and younger than she, including Duncan. Every day he hoped she would be moved to play again.

In the meantime, a fish truck came. For an hour, a man with red gloves stood astride a mountain of ice and shoveled fish out into the baskets borne by the joyful crowd. Fish and fish parts rained through the air as if it were New Year's; the silver scales threw out points of light. People feasted. Duncan began to shed layers of clothes. By now he was beginning to feel more at home speaking Chinese, and could at least answer the kinds of questions people typically asked him—had he eaten yet, and did he like salty food or sweet, and was a place clean or dirty. He could buy stamps at the post office; he could bargain over what little there was for sale. Also, he had begun to feel more at home in his apartment, which featured a concrete floor and a hodgepodge of furniture, ranging from an enormous, Art Deco wardrobe with veined mirrors to a blue metal bedstand, spray-painted with panda bears. There was a coal stove, which had not quite warmed the room in the winter but did now; and, to go with it, a maid, Mrs. Su, whose job it was to keep after the coal soot that seemed to settle everywhere.

The furniture and stove and maid were not Duncan's only luxuries. As a foreign expert, the first the Coal Mining Institute had ever had, he also enjoyed the use of a sit-down toilet—not unknown in the rich South, but of note here in the North—and, most impressively of all, a bathtub complete with hot and cold running water. Never mind that the hot water emanated from a tank on the roof, under which Mrs. Su would make a fire half an hour before Duncan's appointed bathtime. The tub with its faucets was nonetheless a fabled fixture on campus, a subject of much rumor, and, for visitors, a must-see.

Duncan had more visitors now. When he posted a sign-up sheet for individual conversational practice, almost all his students came, bearing stories. Many of these involved the Cultural Revolution, during which some of them were struggled against, while others were Red Guards. How could they sit next to one another in class? Yet they did. They were civil; they lent each other blank cassettes. Those who had been made to dig ditches had not forgotten it. They told Duncan of rape and torture; of seeing loved ones blinded, smeared in shit, drowned, driven to suicide.

No, there was no forgetting. How could they forget any of it? The former Red Guards, on the other hand, professed to have forgotten much. They vaguely recalled riding the trains around the country—being out on a lark, seeing new places. None of them admitted to participating in anything ugly; and indeed, at least one of them seemed quite genuinely more interested in magic tricks and Chinese chess than in ongoing revolution. Still, Duncan was amazed and touched by the fantastic restraint that held his classroom together. Wasn't this related to what he had come to China to see? He had not expected that it would be so tinged with sad realism, though—all anyone wanted anymore was to be left alone, that's what the students said. Nor had he expected it to verge so on the surreal. He had thought, naïvely, that it would have more to do with the old noble code of the scholar-officials. A truly antique idea, such as one found preserved via porcelains in museums.

Or was it?

Louise's turn for conversational practice came on the same afternoon as a basketball tournament. The *thud thud thud* of the ball was so loud, Duncan could hardly hear her speak. From time to time, too, the basketball would hit his window grating with a disconcertingly resounding bang. Yet in a way, Duncan was grateful for the commotion, which helped him relax. His heart had pounded so hard at the prospect of a half hour alone with Louise that before she came he had emptied the pencils from his shirt pocket, for fear that they would rattle.

Louise, in contrast, was unfazed.

"How about we play basketball instead of practice English?" she suggested brightly. As if anticipating that possibility, she had braided her hair and looped it over the top of her head like a laurel wreath—the style she usually chose for athletics.

"Absolutely not," he said with mock seriousness.

"Must we have to practice English?"

"Do we have to practice English."

"Do we have to practice English?"

"We do," he said.

A basketball hit the window grating with a particularly loud bang.

"Such a peaceful room," she said, pursing her lips.

He laughed. "Would you like to see the bathub?"

He showed her the tub with the faucets, then poured her a cup of tea and made her tell him something about herself. By then there were only twenty minutes left to her turn. Still, Duncan managed to learn that Louise was a former aristocrat whose grandparents had made a fortune abroad, but whose parents had elected, at considerable personal expense, to return to China, their homeland. Though she was only older than Duncan by a couple of years, she had married twice already, and had lost both husbands—to illness, Duncan gathered. Also, she had a nineteen-year-old daughter in Nanjing; Louise talked about her with the kind of fretful pride Duncan associated with the wives of astronauts on space missions. Duncan learned that Louise was unusually acquainted with the world, having lived in Germany and France; and, interestingly, that her family had not been struggled against during the Cultural Revolution. "I protected them," she said. She did not volunteer how. Just when Duncan was about to ask, a basketball crashed so hard against the window grate that the windowpane shook.

"Look—the metal is—how do you say? —bended," she said.

"Bent," he said. "The metal is bent."

A knock on the door; the next student, already. It was up to Duncan to imagine, later, how Louise had managed to protect her family—to imagine her calmly confronting an angry crowd, like Gary Cooper, say, in *High Noon*. How easily he could see the mesmerized crowd melting magically away before her! Never mind that in picturing this he knew himself to be shamelessly romanticizing her—inflating, no doubt, both her charm and her integrity. Try as he might, he could see nothing in her to disabuse him of his illusions. Just now she was a coal-mining expert—not something she would have chosen to be. Still she had spoken without resentment of her assignment. She had spoken of re-building the country as if it were her own family fallen on hard times.

"How can China go forward?" she had asked, leaning forward herself. She steadied her chin in her hand like an egg in an eggcup. "I try to study hard so that I can help to build up the country, make China strong."

Duncan's last student for the day, Reginald, maintained that there were more and more people in China these days who said one thing even as they did another, and thought a third thing still—the inevitable result of a repressive regime. And Duncan could see that this was probably true, perhaps even of some of his students. Coal mining in China was horrifically dangerous; these students were supposed to go abroad and bring back new, safer techniques. But would they indeed come back? Duncan had to believe that they would—or at least that his favorites would. He trusted Louise, and William, and Alan, and Rhonda, and Reginald.

Was that just because he liked them? As the weeks went on, Duncan spent more and more time with his students. He made dumplings with them. He watched TV with them, helping them translate endless, plodding programs about Buckingham Palace. He discussed world affairs with them. He visited their dorms.

And, best of all, he went on excursions with them, in the ancient, green car he shared with the school leaders. This was the Warsaw, a Polish vehicle whose tires were so bald, they felt silken; whose windshield, which predated curved glass, had a metal seam up the middle. The seats had been lovingly reupholstered with floral-print towels; the steering wheel had been covered with red velvet; and the innards of the machine had likewise been coddled. The driver had once proudly shown Duncan how he had painstakingly fashioned his own replacement springs from heavy-gauge wire.

If only Duncan enjoyed as much control over the contents of the car! Not that Professor Mo proved his inescapable guide on every trip. But Mo took Duncan to task for choosing William instead of himself for an excursion to Confucius's gravesite at Qufu. And regarding Duncan's plan to take Louise with him to climb the holy Buddhist mountain, Tai Shan—did he really think it appropriate to take a woman, alone, with him anywhere?

"I put her name down on the schedule for a turn but meant for her to bring a partner," sighed Duncan—who in truth had half-dreamed some oversight might occur. "Besides, there would have, of course, been the driver."

"May I name myself to be that partner?" said Mo.

"Oh no, no, you are far too busy with important matters," protested Duncan.

"In other words," said Mo, "you would prefer not to have a lightbulb."

Duncan started a little; "lightbulb" was the same term his father used for a chaperone. "You're welcome to come, Professor Mo, but I understand it's quite a climb. I'm not sure I'll make it myself. Haven't you had an operation on your lung? Certainly there will be other opportunities . . ."

Professor Mo studied him openly, smoking. He was wearing a three-piece suit today, the vest of which sported several moth holes. "Of course, you are single man," he said.

"I have a girlfriend," lied Duncan, even as Louise's visage floated before him, complete with cupped chin.

"Perhaps I will accompany you to the mountain base," said Mo. "And then, of course, there is the other excursion."

"What other excursion?"

"To see your relatives."

"Has that been approved?" Duncan had succeeded in contacting his cousin's family by mail a few months before, but had been seeking permission from the provincial and school officials for a visit ever since.

Mo nodded.

"And they have permission, too?"

"Their unit wants them to travel down from Harbin to Beijing, to meet you. That way you will not see their living conditions."

"How typical—wonderful!" said Duncan. "Thank you for your help in arranging this. It was kind of you." He blurted out this last without sarcasm.

"I have not been to Beijing in some years," observed Professor Mo. "It will be pleasant to visit, especially in the spring." He snuffed out his cigarette, then hooked his thumbs in his vest, arms akimbo.

The trip to Tai Shan started off most magically. Professor Mo settled into a marble-floored hotel to recuperate from the drive, which had consisted almost entirely of roads under repair; this left Duncan and Louise and William free to make the climb alone. They stopped in at the enormous temple at the bottom, then began to wend their way uphill. Lilacs bloomed; vendors under pine-bough shelters sold turnips, walnuts, ices, tea. Everywhere there were goats and chickens, sheep and black pigs. Louise and William, equipped with canteens and shoulder bags, proved lively and informative guides. They translated the stone steles left by the many dignitaries and emperors who had journeyed to the mountain to beg a favor of Buddha. They quoted the poet Li Po, arguing about how to convey the meaning and beauty of his lines.

Then the gentle incline abruptly turned into an ascent unlike any Duncan had made before. He had expected woods, streams, pine needle–strewn paths. Mud. Bugs. Fungi. Instead, he was confronted with a formidable series of rough stone steps, ascending straight up a sheer mountain face. This, according to the Buddhists, was the stairway to heaven, and perhaps its purpose was to prevent overcrowding in paradise: The route was relentless, with no shade whatsoever. The sun felt surprisingly low to the earth—close and intense, as if, whatever season it was elsewhere, here it was high summer. Louise and William were prepared for this, having brought a hat and a pair of sunglasses, respectively; both pressed Duncan to borrow their gear. He adamantly refused. A drought was on; every creek, every waterfall was dry. Hands on his complaining thighs, Duncan stopped frequently to catch his breath, and to marvel, panting, at the thousands of little old ladies—the *lao taitai*—who labored alongside him. They were tiny women, dressed in shapeless blue or gray smocks and black cotton pants. Their gray hair was hidden under black kerchiefs or netted in squarish buns, sometimes with flowers or branches stuck in them. Some wore earrings; a few had enormously long fingernails, such as Duncan had thought were no longer permitted. Didn't everyone in China have to work now? And how was it that so many of the women had bound feet? Duncan associated bound feet with cracked, sepia-toned photographs from the nineteenth century. He beheld the women with amazement even as he reasoned that they were probably in their seventies. And they were peasants. Change came slowly in the countryside. But how could they climb this mountain on those feet? That remained a mystery. And why weren't there any men? The women moved slowly, slowly—fanatically—some of them crawling on their hands and knees. They had come, William said, with the idea of climbing all day and all night, that at the top of the mountain, at dawn, as the sun leapt into the sky—and it really did leap, people said—they might look into their hearts, purifying themselves. Then they could make a request of Buddha.

"This is old China," said William. "The government tried to get rid of this kind of superstition. But the old people are hard to change their minds."

"It is hard to change the minds of the old," corrected Duncan automatically.

"It is hard to change the minds of the old," repeated William. "It is hard to change the minds of the old."

"The trouble is they are—how do you say? Have no hope," said Louise.

"Desperate," said Duncan. "The trouble is that they have no hope. They are desperate."

"The trouble is that they have no hope. They are despate."

"Des-per-ate," said Duncan. "Des-per-ate."

A few of the *lao taitai* had younger women with them— presumably their daughters—to support them or fan them or shade them with an umbrella; even the younger women had wizened faces that looked to have been weathered by the centuries. The women stopped frequently to snack on a kind of flat cornmeal cake they had brought, or to kowtow and make offerings to the Buddha in the many little rock caves and wooden temples on the way up. Ducking his head into one of the temples, Duncan was appalled to find that it housed a bonfire so fierce that he did not dare actually step inside the building.

"They burn paper money, send up to the Buddha," explained William placidly.

"That temple is going to burn down," said Duncan. "It's crazy. And look at all that dry scrub nearby. It's dangerous."

"It is an offering," continued William, nonplussed. "For good fortune."

There were three gates on the way up—the First Heavenly Gate, the Middle Heavenly Gate, and the South Heavenly Gate. At the First Heavenly Gate, Duncan was sweating, looking at his watch, making calculations. By the Middle Heavenly Gate, though, he was thinking less of himself and more of the *lao taitai,* many of whom were kowtowing on the stairs, appealing to Buddha for the strength to go on. He wondered how many deaths there were every year on the mountain.

William bought bamboo walking sticks for himself and Louise and Duncan; Louise opened the collar of her peach-colored polyblend shirt. What an unutterably beautiful part of the anatomy the neck was! Especially the base, with its perfectly matched meeting of graceful, strong bones, and adjacent sweet pockets of impossibly vulnerable flesh. Duncan felt a distinct spring of desire. His ex-girlfriend, Alice, used to say that he was perverse in his ardor, that nothing stirred him like the wholly inappropriate situation, and that this was, in keeping with his entire life, a form of escape. Was that true? All Duncan knew was that his desire to touch Louise there, on her handsome clavicles, so overwhelmed him that he had to put his hands in his pockets whenever they stopped. Louise's neck, he noticed, was flushed a roseate color that Alice—a catalog copywriter—would have called "lovemaker's pink."

Louise herself, meanwhile, was growing more gregarious and inquisitive as the climb went on, as if in unbuttoning her top button she had unbuttoned in other ways as well.

"Are you tired?" she asked Duncan repeatedly, almost tenderly. "Go slowly," she enjoined him. "Take it easy."

She began to quiz him about his health. Perhaps she was interested in health in general, because of what had happened to her two husbands. Perhaps she was brushing up on her health-related English. Perhaps he only imagined that she looked at him more and more searchingly as she progressed from questions about his exercise habits—did he get enough exercise, and what kind of exercise did he get, and did he have partners for the forms of exercise that required them—to questions about his nutrition. What did he eat for breakfast? For lunch? For dinner? Did he cook for himself, or was there someone who cooked for him? Louise smiled when he told her that his girlfriend used to cook for him sometimes, and that he sometimes used to cook for her.

"Of course! Nice boy like you has girlfriend," she said.

"Had a girlfriend," said Duncan. Was there a way of saying this without it seeming like a correction? His teacherly air seemed to nose up into the conversation, not unlike a part of his anatomy he was trying to keep under control.

"Had a girlfriend," said Louise, still smiling. "Nice boy like you had a girlfriend."

"Meaning, I don't have one anymore."

"Ah," she said. "I catch your meaning."

"I catch your meaning" was a favorite phrase of the students, which Duncan had worked all semester to try to eradicate. But now he just sighed, and offered no correction. Instead, he said, "We broke up."

"Broke?"

"I don't have a girlfriend anymore."

"Now he has no any girlfriend," put in William, in an explanatory tone.

"No any" was another phrase Duncan had focused on, for months. He felt a rise of irritation. "Now he has no girlfriend," he corrected.

"Who?" said Louise.

"I," said Duncan. "Now I have no girlfriend."

"Broken heart?" she asked, head atilt, chin cupped in hand.

"Broken heart," he affirmed, with a feeling of simultaneous connection and defeat. In fact, he had broken the relationship off, and the heartache, to his surprise, had proven mostly Alice's. But how to explain that? Here he was, the foreign expert, and yet he felt as helpless in his communication as a student.

Louise looked at him sympathetically. Duncan noticed that she had not tied the ribbons of her straw hat, but rather had tucked them, eccentrically, behind her ears, so that they mingled with various loose strands of her hair. Her black hair was gathered today in a low, loose ponytail.

"We are—how do you say?—comrades," she said then, firmly; at which point, William, in distraction or discretion, turned his head as she quickly, consolingly squeezed Duncan's hand.

Did William see that squeeze? It was hard to tell, what with the sunglasses. Quite possibly the good soul was too preoccupied with the role of guide to think of much besides how best to provide for his teacher's comfort.

"May I offer you a cup of tea?" he asked. "Would you care for a piece of sorghum candy?"

They climbed on. Now, walking stick in hand, William led their party. This meant that Louise followed a bit behind him, and that Duncan, happily, followed a few paces behind her. For a while, he watched the swing of her ponytail—how part of it nestled inside her collar and part swung loose, fanning itself over the cloth of her shirt. But slowly, inevitably, his interest drifted downward. He was not the kind of man who spent his time looking down women's blouses and up their skirts. Who could climb steps behind a female form for hour upon hour, though, and not notice the tightening and loosening of her gray slacks across her buttocks, the working of the pant legs in and out of her crotch? He examined the creasing of the cloth, the strain of a certain seam. He watched a sweat diamond grow larger. What had she meant when she said they were comrades? Finally tiring herself, she began to rest one hand behind her back, delineating the extraordinarily graceful line of her waist. She leaned on her walking stick, readjusted her canteen, her shoulder bag. Several times she even flapped the hem of her shirt a little, to cool herself—an unconscious act, he assumed; what an intimacy it seemed, to be privy to a moment when she had forgotten herself. Alice had never forgotten herself. Alice had been utterly witty and composed, except when she was having her nervous breakdowns.

It seemed an intimacy, too, the several times Louise and Duncan stopped, to be flushed and panting together.

"Stop, William," they called at one point. But he did not hear them and ploughed steadily ahead.

"He is a water buffalo," said Louise, looking up.

"Look back," said Duncan. "Look how far we've come."

She turned. "Oh," she said. "It makes me dizzy." She bowed her head; a stray breeze came up; her hat tumbled down a few steps, landing at the knees of a struggling *lao taitai*. Duncan retrieved it, considering his little gallantry with some irony. What did it say about him that he chose to help lithe Louise instead of the old woman? He was glad this old woman at least had, not one, but two younger women with her.

"Are you all right?" he asked Louise, and almost placed her hat on her head; but she blushed so hard that he handed it to her instead.

Did she regret squeezing his hand as she had?

"I am in excellent health," she answered, replacing her hat ribbons behind her ears. "How about you?"

"I, too, am in excellent health."

"Good." Smiling her pursed smile, she squeezed his hand again. "Have you had any big sickness?" she asked as she resumed climbing.

The crowds of *lao taitai* continued their inexorable way up the mountain. The steps were steeper now, and so crudely made that

Duncan found himself concentrating a little less on Louise's posterior and more on his footing—so much so that when William suddenly appeared, Duncan startled.

"We are almost at the top," said William. "I come back down to make report."

The few scattered bushes at the top of the mountain were abloom with rocks. Those were prayers, William explained. The *lao taitai* threw the rocks into the bushes; if the rocks stuck, it meant the prayers would be answered. Besides the rock bushes there was real rock—no trees—and a hostelry, into which William checked himself, Duncan, and Louise. The hostel was a basic affair, and yet a luxury difficult to enjoy. How could Duncan sleep in a warm, soft bed when those pilgrims who were not still climbing all night were going to be sleeping on the ground? Duncan asked if he couldn't give his room up to some of the old women, but William's answer was a laugh.

"You are foreign expert," he said. "The hotel will make report about you. Can they write you slept outside on the ground? Impossible!"

Still Duncan mulled over matters of birth and happenstance, as in the smoke-filled dining room he tried to elbow his way to a dinner of bean sprouts and steamed rolls. The *lao taitai* proved surprisingly aggressive. They grabbed food right out of his hands; they demanded that he give up his seat that they might sit down. So pushy were they about the latter especially that Duncan found himself, to his surprise, shaking his head no. Hadn't he just been thinking about giving his hostel room up to the *lao taitai*? Yet he would not give his seat up to them. He shook his head almost as adamantly as did William and Louise. On the other hand, for what it was worth, he felt a renewed sympathy for the *lao taitai* when he left the dining hall and noticed how precipitously the temperature had dropped since nightfall. How many of the old women had brought jackets with them? Blankets? None, apparently. Yet it was cold enough now to set a person's teeth on edge, and a formidable wind had risen, with great broadsiding gusts.

What with the drought, the hotel was out of water, but Duncan and his students each had a full canteen; in his private room, Duncan slipped into sleep provisioned. Still, his sleep was fitful at best as he dreamt of dropping things, some of them quietly, some with a loud clang. Another loud clang—no, a loud clanging. A bell; voices; people running up and down the hall. Now he was awake. Shouting, swearing, banging. He thought the voices were saying "fire"; and when he peered out the clear streak in his white-washed window, sure enough, there it was—a broad sulfur yellow glow, gently curved at the bottom, like a picture of the surface of the sun from a text on the solar system. Those bonfires in the temple, he thought. He dressed, shaking. Outside his door, he waited for Louise and William. The courtyard was in a flurry. Only the moon was itself, overhead as always, implacable and still, its brilliant light reassuringly hard white—the proper color of night lighting. Duncan clutched his water canteen, feeling the dig of its webbed strap in his shoulder, the cool of its metal belly against his hand. He could hear his mother's voice. *What do you mean, you died in China?* Leave it to him to die the wrong way, Duncan thought. Arnie would no doubt manage to drop dead in front of the swankest funeral parlor in town.

The fire burned through the night. William kept saying that there was no danger, that the top of the mountain was solid rock, but it was hard not to worry that they would all be asphyxiated by the smoke when it blew their way. The smoke was thick enough to obscure the moon, and the people, too, so that they instinctively began to wail in the billowing blackness like riders on a roller coaster, plummeting downhill. The wind, the wind. Even more than the people on the mountaintop seemed at the mercy of the fire, they seemed at the mercy of the wind. Another gust; the *lao taitai* wailed again. Duncan envied them their keening release as, flanked by Louise and William, he watched the fire silently from a perch on a large rock. In America, there might be a rescue attempt, with helicopters. In America, there might be a fire-fighting attempt, too, unless the fire had been deemed part of the mountain's natural cycle, essential to the survival of, say, a certain charcoal-eating beetle. Here there was nothing to be attempted. Even if fire trucks could make it safely up the road to the Middle Heavenly Gate—Duncan had learned there was indeed a road that far—what could they do? Especially with no streams to pump from. There was only the fire, still burning; and the wind, still howling. Louise sat closer to Duncan than did William, but even William sat close enough that Duncan could feel the warmth of his body, and appreciate the shelter he provided from that wind. William wore his canteen hanging straight down from his neck; Duncan wore his the same way. As for Louise—how hard it was not to put his arm around hatless Louise, whose canteen lay on the ground; who was shivering. He had started to, at one point, but she had seemed to stiffen and move away. Was that because of William? And why should they care, if they were going to die? He should sweep her up in his arms, and take her into his room. They should throw off their shackles, and live these few moments in freedom. As the night went on, he resolved over and over to do it—to live. He recalled scenes from *Last Tango in Paris,* from *Swept Away.* He wondered how old Louise had been when she lived in France, and what movies she had seen. He pictured scenes in which she lay on a beach, or arched back against a garden wall. He pictured her pelvic bones, as beautiful as her clavicles; he envisioned the adjacent vulnerable flesh. Her hair spread around her, unbraided, undone; she offered her hard-nippled breasts to him. He imagined sucking, biting, sweating; imagined her impatient, then languid, then impatient once more.

But when he looked over at the woman at his side, these visions seemed tawdry and insufficient, the stuff of a schoolboy's wet dreams. For Louise seemed to believe either that they were going to live, or else that she should die according to the code by which she had lived. Not that she said so. She simply sat in silence, staring at the fire, thinking thoughts Duncan could not fathom. She was, he knew, a physical woman, a woman unafraid of sweat; a woman who had fallen in love and married twice. A woman ardent in all things. And she liked him. When he had drunk the last of his canteen, she automatically took it from him, leapt to the ground, and replenished it from her own. He protested; she clasped his hand for a third time, to silence him. But that was all. Beyond that, she only waited to know what was to come and, with something like nobility, chose to do nothing.

Still the fire burned. But the hostel did not burn, and no one was asphyxiated; and slowly, finally, the fire began to peter out. A scrub fire, that's what Duncan learned to call it later. A scrub fire, perhaps blown out by the wind. The yellow that was the mountainside began to fade to a wheaten color—the color of dry grass—just as the sky began to lighten, so that it seemed as if the fire had risen up and been absorbed into the atmosphere—as if there were no real division between heaven and earth. How movingly magnificent was the heave of clearing land, as it came into view: an expanse of purple crags and mist-sunk valleys—an unpeopled sweep, the province of swift clouds and gods. It did seem the province of gods. Then the moment the *lao taitai* had come for was upon them. The wind seemed to die down completely as the sun came up—jumping little jumps, just as it was supposed to, a leap leap leap into the sky; and for a long moment, there was holiness on the mountain. In the pure calm, Duncan felt a twinge of envy for the *lao taitai,* who did not seem desperate at all, but at peace, full of an old, large faith that would never live for him. It was he who was desperate—godless, modern man, whose most stirring visions came from sex scenes in movies. He looked on the blackened mountain, visible now with the risen sun. Then he closed his eyes with the other pilgrims and found, to his surprise, that he had much in his heart. For what was he but a free man who had rejected much and embraced little? He was a free man who had never truly loved. He was a free man who believed nothing in particular, who did nothing in particular. He was a free man who had not even embraced his freedom.

He was a long time opening his eyes.

When finally he did, he found that many of the *lao taitai* had gone to breakfast, and that William had gone for a walk, but that Louise remained beside him. Duncan turned to her.

"Did you ask the Buddha for something?" she asked.

He hesitated. "I asked the Buddha that I might find love." In fact, he had not asked for anything, exactly; but he realized now, accepted now, that he was speaking in a kind of translation. One had to be willing to do that, to begin with, if one were to tangle with the world.

"I asked the Buddha to introduce you to someone special."

"Do I not know someone special?"

She stood up. Her feet angled downward on the sloping rock as, arms spread, she sprang to the ground, graceful as Peter Pan. For all the trials of the long night, her blouse looked surprisingly fresh and unwrinkled, as did she.

"Your canteen," he said, handing it to her.

"You know no one," she said mysteriously. "Wait and see." Then, hanging her canteen back around her neck, she added, "Be careful about William."

Louise did not come to class the next day, and the day after that was reported gone altogether. Gone home, people said. Applied for home leave and got it. They seemed mostly amazed that Louise had managed to get her unit to agree to let her travel on such short notice. Must have some string somewhere, they said, giving Duncan a funny look. William especially seemed to steer clear of Duncan. Only with great effort did Duncan manage to corner him and ask what was going on, to which William answered that in China, these days, it was better to avoid standing in a stable for fear of smelling of shit.

"You are a foreigner," he said. "Better not to be involved."

"Did you make a report?" asked Duncan.

"I am class monitor."

"What did you say? In your report."

William looked away. " 'Honesty is best policy.' Isn't that what you teach us? An American saying? I am not clever man, know all kinds of back door. I am simple man. But I am honest, all my life, since I was born."

"You are a spy." Duncan regretted his words as soon as he said them.

"I am no spy," William said. "I am just honest." And again, "I am class monitor."

The weather turned almost as hot and dry as it had been on Tai Shan. Mrs. Su reported that her husband had begun sleeping on the floor, now that it was too hot for them both to sleep with their child on the bed. The time had come, too, she said, to hang mosquito netting. On the streets, women carrying their vegetables in plastic net bags hugged the walls as they walked, trying to stay in the shade. The wind blew up enormous clouds of dust. Duncan's ears were gritty with it; he was forced to keep his apartment windows shut, as if it were winter. The campus electricity went out regularly. No one played basketball. No one came to visit. Duncan kept to himself. Though Louise, worryingly, did not reappear, he said nothing. From time to time he thought about the climb up Tai Shan, and about the fire, and about the holy moment at dawn, and about how changed he had felt by it all—how full of possibility, as if he were on the brink of living a new life. But now he did not feel changed at all—unless he were to count, that is, finding himself more prickly about his authority. When a student questioned his grading on an exam, he found himself answering more curtly than necessary. He also noticed that he gave more dictations, strolling up and down the aisles of the classroom like an old-fashioned drillmaster.

When it came time to make his trip to Beijing, he was glad to be getting away.

From the moment they boarded the train, though, Professor Mo proved an insufferable companion.

"So the star has faded," he said, tea in one hand, cigarette in the other. "Once a beloved teacher, not so beloved now."

"I was never trying to be popular," said Duncan.

"That's good. For who stands by you now?" Mo laughed, drinking his tea, in a gulp, down to a bed of leaves. "No one stands by anyone. That was the lesson I learned in years past, and it's still true."

"Thank you for sharing your wisdom."

"How kind of me."

"How impossibly kind." Duncan gazed out the window at the flicker of fields without end. His own tea remained untouched on the doilied flip-up table before him. "Do you know where Louise went?" he asked finally. "And how did she manage to get her unit to send her home?"

"She was summoned home for immoral behavior," said Mo, lighting a cigarette with an old silver lighter. "I wrote the report."

"What did you write?" asked Duncan. "How would you even know what to write? You were in the hotel. She did absolutely nothing even slightly immoral."

"Either I knew or I guessed," said Mo. "Either it was indeed quite true or else quite false. Either William made a report or he didn't. I will tell you, though. Louise talks more in Chinese than in English. She is a clever girl, from a rich family. I knew her father. He made a fortune smuggling drill bits for making machine guns in World War Two. German drill bits, the best in the world, made of a special steel. Whom were they coming from? Whom were they going to? Why did they have to go from Manchuria to Beijing to Shanghai to Hanoi to Chongqing? He chose not to know. Those drill bits were worth ten times their weight in gold back then. It's a talented family. During the Cultural Revolution, they were not struggled against. How did that happen? you may ask. You may be surprised. But you should not be surprised." He held his cigarette delicately, like a scientific specimen, pinched between his thumb and forefinger. "It's a talented family."

In Beijing, Duncan trudged from the Forbidden Palace to the Summer Garden to the Temple of Heaven. Carvings, marble. Dynasties, intrigue. Emperors, concubines, history. Great quantities of history, complete with historical implications. The history cheered him somewhat. Still, on the second day he claimed to be sick and stayed in the hotel, as he did on the third day. Professor Mo called a doctor, who diagnosed Duncan, via his pulse, as too *yang*. Duncan's body had too much heat, he said. Duncan needed cooling foods, like mung bean soup, or seaweed, or chrysanthemum tea. Duncan also needed an herbal remedy. The doctor wrote out a prescription, which Mo dutifully went to fill.

And so it was that Duncan was blissfully alone when the front desk called to say that his cousin was in the lobby.

"Duncan?"

"Guotai?"

"Nice to meet you, nice to meet you!"

Guotai had the family dimples, which had always mortified Duncan, and also the square family jaw, of which Duncan had felt rather proud. He looked to be some ten or fifteen years older than Duncan, though; and where Duncan was of medium height and stocky, Guotai was tall for a Chinese man, and spindly. A bend in his torso gave him a hinged look in profile, as if he had been designed to fold up. He held the palms of his hands in the small of his back, seemingly to prevent this eventuality. He had very little hair, some of it black, some of it brown, some of it white; his skin was pitted; and he smiled a broad smile of rotten teeth as he described how he had ridden down hard-seat from Harbin to Beijing for this visit. Twelve hours, he said. His teeth were yellow or blue-gray and looked as if they had no enamel, yet they were hardly as alarming as his cough. Nothing serious, he insisted, hacking, though he also mentioned that he had not brought his wife because she had TB.

Duncan considered how close one should stand to someone who might have TB.

"And who is this?" Duncan indicated the child by his cousin's side.

"What you say?" demanded Guotai of his child in English. "What you say?"

The child—a large-headed boy of about seven—hung his head. He, too, had the family dimples and jaw; Duncan wondered for the first time what it would be like to have a son. The child looked healthier than his father, though just as skinny. He had a crew cut, and large dull eyes, and a scar across one cheek. When he looked up, it was to lift his upper lip in a snarl. He was missing two teeth.

"What you say? Huh? No face. Come on now."

"Nice meet you."

Guotai smiled. "You see his English how good. What you say next?"

"I good boy. Never make trouble."

"I train him," boasted Guotai. "Give him lesson every day."

"What's his name?" asked Duncan.

"What your name?" said Guotai.

The child snarled again, pulling at his shirt. A square of light from the window fell on the outstretched fabric. He gazed at it as if in a mirror.

"What your name!" said Guotai.

"Bing Bing."

"You speak such good English, Bing Bing," said Duncan.

Bing Bing let go of his shirt and stopped snarling. "If I go to United States, I no trouble." He stuck his tongue out through the gap in his teeth.

"Stupid!" said Guotai. Then, as the child recoiled: "My father, mother have big trouble, you know. We were struggle against. I raise this boy by sell matches on the street. We have no cooking oil. We have no place to live. We have no coat to wear. In springtime we ate tree leaves. Even today I have no job. My wife is sick now. How can we live?" He coughed and coughed.

"We'd better talk upstairs," said Duncan.

. . .

"He needs to see a doctor," Duncan told Professor Mo later. "He's sick. I think he has TB."

"That cough," said Professor Mo. "Terrible."

"Is that why you left right after I introduced you?"

"A cleverer reaction, perhaps, than inviting him to your room."

"I didn't know what else to do. He kept insisting he was fine."

"You are lucky he has TB. That way, the government will tell him he cannot go to the United States. Otherwise, you will be required to tell him yourself. After all, a man like that, who is going to give him a job? A man like that, how can you let him come live in your house?"

"I don't know what you mean," said Duncan; although in fact, for once, he did.

To begin with, there had been the cough.

"I don't have TB," said Guotai, over and over, so that Duncan had tried not to turn his head every time Guotai began hacking. On the other hand, Duncan had been anxious not to catch TB himself.

"You don't believe me," said Guotai sadly. "You turn your head. You think I have TB. But why I should lie? A strong man like me."

Also, there were the stories. It had seemed to Duncan that he had heard every horror story the Cultural Revolution could produce from his students; and indeed, nothing Guotai had to say about what he had been through—the famines, the shortages, the beatings, the prison camps—seemed entirely new. At the same time, it was worse, because of the outcome. Duncan's students had all gone on to become part of a new elite. Guotai, on the other hand, had emerged not even a bitter man, like Professor Mo, but a broken one. He had been reduced to begging. He had lived for many years on the street. Who knew what would have happened to him and his family if his wife had not at least been given that job in a factory? That was just three years ago. Her class background, thankfully, was a little less bad than his. Also, her father had not deserted the army, as had Guotai's.

"They ask my father go fight in Korea," said Guotai. "At first he say yes. He has no choice. But then time to kill somebody, and he cannot. Instead, he cry. He say he love peace so much, he name his son Guotai. That is me. My name means 'country peace.' He say he must go home, all his plants waiting. Of course, the army kill him for go home just like that. First they kill him, and then the government try to kill my mother. Until one day, she is dead. Then try to kill me."

"What do you mean, try to kill your mother?" asked Duncan.

"No food coupon, no room to live, no job," said Guotai. "That's how they try. My mother die right after my father. At that time I am seven, like Bing Bing. But here I am today, still live."

Duncan smiled, feeling for a moment his cousin's triumph, even as he made some calculations and realized, with a start, that Guotai was not in his forties or fifties, but about the same age as he was. That meant that the whole time he, Duncan, was eating hot dogs and learning to ride a bike, his cousin was an orphan on the street. While Duncan was reading novels like *Oliver Twist,* Guotai was actually begging and freezing and starving. Duncan tried to imagine what Arnie's reaction to his cousin would be. Would Arnie ever wonder what Duncan and he had done to be born to their father, and not to their father's brother? And how much did their father know about what had gone on? *So many cousins, who can keep track of them all?* he had said when Duncan told him he was looking for the address of the one cousin still in China. What his father had turned up for Duncan was not Guotai's address, which none of the relatives seemed to have, but the name of the factory where Guotai's wife worked. This someone had given Duncan's father's number-four sister, who lived in Idaho. *I don't know what the wife is doing there. Maybe some kind of technical work,* Duncan's aunt had said.

Guotai's coughing began again. Duncan concentrated on not turning his head. He tried, too, not to take note of the places his cousin spat, when he spat on the floor. When his cousin asked for food and gifts, Duncan tried to provide them without judgment.

Impossible to overlook, though, was the haranguing of the child. Bing Bing, having never seen a bathroom before, peed into the floor grate. He also moved his bowels there, only to have his father hit him so hard, he fell into the bathtub.

"Stupid!" he told his son.

"It's all right," said Duncan, but still Guotai raised his hand to hit his son again.

"Stupid!"

"He didn't know," said Duncan.

"He should ask. Stupid!"

Bing Bing sniveled. Duncan tried to suggest that Guotai might be gentler with the child.

"His mother spoil him," Guotai explained blithely. "I make sure he is afraid of someone."

"In America, we don't treat children that way," said Duncan. Then: "If you came to America, you would have to stop."

He stopped. "If I come to America?"

Immediately, Duncan realized he had made a mistake in raising the subject. Still, he nodded.

"Who stop me?"

"The government."

"The government?" Guotai was so amazed that for a moment

he could say nothing. "You mean, United States government worse than Chinese government?"

"In this way—you might think so. Yes."

"If I come to United States, I stop," he said. "My English so good, I no trouble, you know. Bing Bing, too. I am strong man, healthy."

But he did not stop that afternoon. When Duncan gave Bing Bing an apple and Bing Bing dropped it, Guotai hit him again.

"Stupid!"

"It's all right. I'll get him another one," said Duncan.

"He eat this one, okay."

"But it's dirty," said Duncan. The apple had fallen right into one of the islands of spittle Guotai had left on the wooden floor.

"No dirty," said Guotai. Using a coffee cup as a basin, he rinsed the apple off with orange soda, then handed it back to his child. "This boy no trouble. When he go to America, you will see."

"You are going to have to leave them both here," said Professor Mo. "Of course. You are foreign expert. You have things to do in America. If your cousin has TB, you have to tell him to go save himself. Every man for himself! In America, in China, it's the same. Every man for himself!"

"Would you like to join us for dinner?" asked Duncan politely. "We're going to the Duck House."

"Perhaps another time," said Mo.

"Ah," said Duncan.

"After all, my foreign expert is sick all day, cannot go sight-seeing. I have to buy medicine, make report."

"I understand. There are so many important matters. It's a real problem."

"It is. But what can I do?" Mo flung his arm with some exuberance over the back of his chair even as he shook his head in resignation.

On the walk to the restaurant, Guotai mentioned the United States in every other sentence. This was Duncan's fault, of course. Still he felt as though he were in the dining hall at the top of Tai Shan again, being pushed by *lao taitai*. He wondered where Louise was, and whether she had returned to school. And why did she put her hat ribbons behind her ears? He wanted to ask her why, and to tie the ribbons under her chin for her, and to show her how much less likely her hat was to blow off if she tied it on. He imagined her laughing at these little attentions. He imagined her drawing his face toward hers, into the lovely wedge of shade under her hat's wide brim.

"What was your mother like?" Duncan asked Guotai, trying to move the conversation onto a new plane.

"My mother was good woman," said Guotai. "A—what do you call?—a saint. All her life she suffer, and when she die, she say to me one thing."

"What was that?"

" 'Go to United States.' She say, 'Promise me you go to United States. Ask your cousin to help you.' "

"She said that?"

"She did," insisted Guotai, coughing.

"But she didn't even know you had any cousins."

"Your father wrote letter. She knew."

"And wouldn't she have told you to ask my father to help you?" Now they were in front of the restaurant. "She wouldn't have told you to ask me. I was just a child then. She would've told you to ask my father."

"She say that, too. She say, 'Ask your cousins. Ask your uncle.' She say, 'They will help you.' "

"She would have first said to ask your uncle, and then she would have said to ask your cousins, if she mentioned the cousins at all. And why would she have told you to ask her husband's brother? What about her own brothers and sisters? Wouldn't she have told you to ask them?"

"Why you ask me these questions? How you know what my mother say? It was long time ago." Guotai coughed.

Duncan turned his head.

"I do not have TB," said Guotai.

"What's that cough, then?"

"I have a cold."

"We had better get you some cold medicine."

Guotai put his hands to his back, mustering his pride. "I think Bing Bing and me go back to Harbin now. We waste our time here. Why should we go to America anyway, become rich American who never help anybody? Better go home see my wife before she die."

At this Duncan softened, and insisted Guotai and Bing Bing at least stay for dinner.

"Smell the duck," he said. "Come on. Are you going to make me eat by myself? You can't get a train tonight anyway."

Guotai thanked Duncan several times as the meal progressed, in its elaborate way, through various duck parts, up to the duck skin. It was not a meal he was likely to have a chance to eat ever again, he said, and he was glad Bing Bing was having a chance to experience it, too.

"He remember this when he is old man," said Guotai. "Both of us will remember for a long time."

Between thanks, though, he was surly. "You turn your head," he told Duncan, coughing. "I told you before, don't turn your head."

"Why would I have dinner with you at all if I thought you had TB?" said Duncan—reflecting that this was, in truth, a good question.

Guotai heaped his plate with stir-fried duck innards.

Bing Bing, meanwhile, began to squirm. *"I can't eat any more,"* he announced in Chinese. *"I'm full."*

"Delicious special food like this, of course you have room for more," answered Guotai ferociously, also in Chinese. He seemed about to hit Bing Bing as usual, but stopped himself. *"You know, children in America don't get hit. That's what your uncle here says."*

Bing Bing's eyes widened.

"Some children do," conceded Duncan, the only one speaking in English. "But most don't."

"You hear that?" said Guotai.

"But we are not going to America."

"That is true, too," said Guotai. *"We have no one to help us because we are poor and I have a cold."* He smiled his lusterless smile. *"However, we are having this nice dinner. Have a Coke."* He pushed a bottle toward his son.

"I want a beer," said Bing Bing.

"Then have a beer," said Guotai.

"He drinks beer?" said Duncan, amazed.

Guotai laughed, pouring the remains of a beer can into a mostly empty soda glass. *"Of course he drinks beer. In Harbin, everyone drinks beer. The average is twelve bottles per person per day. We are so close to Russia, you see. They taught us everything we know. To the Russians, those drunks!"* He lifted his own glass as Bing Bing, with two hands, lifted his. *"Bottoms up!"*

Duncan watched, aghast, as Bing Bing chugged his drink. The

child's face was so small that the rim of the glass almost touched his eyebrows. "Can he really hold his liquor? At that age?"

"Of course! Of course!" Guotai pushed another glass across to his son. *"Show your uncle what you can do."*

Bing Bing, elbows in the air, dutifully chugged a second beer. When he emerged from behind the glass, the gap in his teeth was filled with foam.

"If he drinks enough, he'll dance on the table," promised Guotai.

"That's more than enough," said Duncan. "Don't give him any more. Look at his face. Look at how red he is. Look at his eyes. He's drunk."

"More beer!" said Bing Bing.

"No more beer," said Duncan. "You know, in America, children don't drink beer."

"He says in America, children don't drink beer," said Guotai.

"But we're in China. We're not going to America. More beer! More beer!"

"No more beer," said Duncan. "It's not good for you."

Guotai poured another glass.

"Stop," said Duncan. He grabbed his cousin's arm. "I said stop."

"What's the matter, are you afraid he will embarrass you the way we would embarrass you if we came to the United States? Don't worry, nobody here will even care. This is China. He can dance on the table and nobody will say anything. Who wants to look for trouble? Better not to get involved, that's how Chinese people think. Sweep the snow from your own doorstep."

Bing Bing, meanwhile, was indeed climbing up onto the table.

"Stop!" said Duncan. "Stop!"

But Bing Bing was dancing on the white tablecloth. " 'We all live in the yellow submarine, yellow submarine, yellow submarine,' " he sang. " 'We all live . . .' "

"Good dancing, good dancing!" cried Guotai. *"Show him what his Chinese cousins are! Embarrass him to death! He's here to visit China—show him what our country is. In China, you can dance, you can starve. Still people act as if they do not even see you! Show him! You watch."* Guotai turned to Duncan, his eyes glittering strangely. *"This is China! Nobody will say anything! You watch!"*

But he was wrong. In fact, a hostess was already headed their way with a frown on her face when Bing Bing passed out and fell into the tureen of duck soup.

On the train back to school, Duncan said nothing.

"I heard about your party," said Professor Mo.

Duncan looked out the window.

"What a distinguished family you have."

Duncan looked at the floor.

"If you start to cough, let me know right away."

"I called a doctor for my cousin before we left."

"How interesting. Also, no doubt, you gave him money."

"I'm going to adopt that child," announced Duncan, though in fact he had not decided what to do. In fact, he wasn't even sure a single man could legally adopt a child, much less that Guotai or Bing Bing would agree to such a move. Still, it was what he wished to do. Or, more accurately: He wished to be the sort of person who would adopt a child like Bing Bing. A wise person, who understood what he owed fate, and how to acknowledge that. A noble person, who in another time might have become a scholar-official. But was he that person? And if he was, why did he feel as though he needed to lie down and sleep for a long, long time?

"How interesting," said Mo again. "Has your cousin graciously agreed to accept your kindness?"

Duncan did not answer.

"I'm so surprised." Mo made a loopy movement with his foot, happy and full of triumph. "Perhaps you should head back to the United States right after you're done teaching, instead of traveling around. So you can work on the adoption."

Duncan said nothing to this, either, not wanting to agree with Professor Mo, though in fact he was indeed thinking about cutting his leave short. There were too many truths here. He wanted to go home. This is what he knew: That the weather was extreme in China. That he missed pizza. That he envied his brother Arnie, with his sense of purpose in life. How shallow it was, to believe in making money; and yet how it protected one against life itself— disorienting, disconcerting life. It was as useful as religion. Perhaps it was a religion, to which he, Duncan, should convert. For Louise had her code; the old women on Tai Shan had their belief; even Professor Mo had his vengeful calculation. What did Duncan have with which to organize pointless, brutal life? He had rejected his old code of rejection, and rightly so; but now more than ever he could only cry to think of those Sung dynasty vases, all that certainty behind glass.

Perhaps he was just another idealist on a road to end badly, like Professor Mo, or his uncle.

So he thought before he arrived back at the Coal Mining Institute. But then there, waiting at the door of his apartment, magical as a spot of moonlight in the middle of the day, were Louise and what appeared to be her younger self—an impossibly lovely girl, very like her mother, only in finer form. Louise's agility was, in her, grace; Louise's radiance was, in her, luminosity. Out of turquoise comes blue, that's what the Chinese said. Louise's daughter had the sort of classic beauty around which hushes fell and plots rose. There was no real goodness in looks; Duncan knew that. And yet the gentle perfection of her cheekbones, of her eyebrows, of her eyes and mouth, of her utterly diaphanous complexion—how it moved him all the same. It gave one hope that from the messy world might occasionally arise clarity; that poise and harmony were part of the natural order of things. Duncan could only imagine how protective Louise had had to be of her daughter; how much trouble she might have already attracted. Was Duncan the man who could shelter her? And could he do this for Louise, for love—learn to love her daughter instead of herself? Perhaps he was getting ahead of himself. And yet how he adored Louise already for wanting such a thing, if that's what she wanted. How he adored her for wanting more—he hoped she wanted more—than for him to sponsor her daughter to the United States.

"Hello," said Louise. She was wearing the same peach-colored blouse she had worn climbing Tai Shan. The top button was buttoned now, but the blouse still appeared as preternaturally fresh as ever.

"Hello," said Duncan. "How is your health?"

"I am in good health," she said. "And you?"

"I am healthy, too. And who is this?"

"I like to introduce to you the someone special," said Louise.

"I'd like to introduce to you someone special," corrected Duncan.

"No," said Louise. "The someone special. Remember? I promise you. On the mountain."

"I do remember. This is your daughter?"

"My daughter, Lingli."

"Hello," said Duncan.

"Nice to meet you," said Lingli. Her voice was low but clear—a guileless, confident voice.

"She speaks English," said Louise. "Better than her mother."

In other words, she can go to the United States, Duncan almost said. But he held his tongue.

Louise said, "I told her you are a good man."

"Ah," he joked. "You made a report."

"I don't catch your meaning."

Had Louise startled? "You made a report," he repeated carefully. "About me."

"No report," said Louise. "What report?"

"I just meant about me, to your daughter. You made a report to your daughter."

"I thought you ask if I made a report to Professor Mo."

"Of course you didn't," he said. "Why would I ask that?"

"I bring you my daughter," said Louise. "All the way from Nanjing. Her name is Lingli."

"Yes, we've met."

Louise's daughter looked at her mother with consternation, turning her face from Duncan. Her delicate brow rumpled. A shadow cast a hard line across the exquisite undulation of her cheek.

More gently, he said, "You've come all the way from Nanjing. How was the train ride?"

Louise looked at Lingli. "You say."

"Perfectly comfortable," said Lingli.

"It's a long ride all the same," he said.

"Do you have something more to say?" said Louise.

"It was not long at all," said Lingli. "It was perfectly comfortable."

"Perhaps you'll both come in and rest?" said Duncan. And again: "You've come all the way from Nanjing."

Louise hesitated, touching her chin. Her head listed; her face reddened as though she were going to cry. "I've made a big mistake. How do you say? A terrible mistake. I've make a terrible mistake."

"Please," he said then. "No mistake."

"A mistake," she insisted. "My meaning is . . ."

"Please. I understand your meaning," he said. "No mistake. I'm sorry. I'm the one who's made mistakes. Please."

And with that, he unlocked his door, marveling at how it seemed, with no effort at all, to open wide. It was possible Louise had made many reports. It was possible that she came, after all, from a most talented family. It was possible she was sorry; it was possible she wasn't; it was possible she loved him herself; it was possible she didn't love him at all. It was possible that he would never love her daughter, or that her daughter would never love him. It was possible her daughter would make reports, too. It was possible he could never forgive himself if he sponsored Lingli to the United States and left poor Guotai and Bing Bing behind. How tangled up everything was already. Still he could say this, that there was one thing he had, being an American—not so much an unshakable conviction as a habit of believing in the happiest possibility. Truly it was a form of blindness. He understood why denizens of the Old World laughed at people like him. Yet he saw now, finally, that it was as incurably his as any faith. For how noble Louise's daughter seemed to him, how pure an expression of everything elegant and upright about China! And how easily, still, despite all he had been through, he could see the proper end to his hopelessly tortured story. He offered Lingli a seat. Heart throbbing, he offered to show her his bathtub. For there she was, his heart's leading lady. How vividly he could imagine the scenes and the credits; and, after the credits, the applause.

JUST WAIT

Any reasonable baby shower would have properly culminated in the video recorder with the instant-playback feature. The present was addressed to The Formerly Thin Addie Wing from her three tactless brothers, and arrived suspiciously wrapped in a brown paper grocery bag. There was no box or warranty card. If the camera was hot, nobody said so. As for the bag, this was fastened with an antique diaper pin, courtesy of Addie's number-two brother, Billy, who was Mr. Flea Market in the family as a result of having gone to prep school. No one could explain it, but that's what had happened. He had gone in wearing Nike everything, thanks to money he had made with his paper route, and had come out a 1930s North Woods type who read Herodotus by lantern light. Billy could ice-fish. He talked suddenly slowly. He left off talking after making his point. That proved the most dramatic change, and the most unnerving, especially as he kept it up all through college and on into what was apparently his adulthood. Now he was forty-two and still doing it.

To be fair, Addie thought that the outdoorsy persona was about embarrassment. He was embarrassed to have turned even more thoughtful than he had been before. He had always been a guy who sought the bottom of things, as if there were a bottom that could be found—as if people could do more in life than paw down through one viscous reality into another mess. Addie found this charming. She herself knew what it was to wade into a field full of lupine and be filled with wonderment. Once, too, in a rogue storm on a mountaintop, she had dropped to her knees and prayed—not knowing what else to do in the onslaught of water and wind—and the extremis of that moment had stayed with her. She recalled the cold press of the hard stone, and the rain running from her clumped hair; she remembered the sky—brutal, power-mad, dead to mercy. And, recalling those things, she understood Billy's hunting and fishing clothes. They were his way of saying he didn't belong to the quotidian world. He belonged to the world of transcendence, like a priest.

But Addie's stepbrother, Mark, liked to say that Billy—Will, he called himself now, had in fact called himself for some twenty-odd years—looked as though he had lent L. L. Bean his first tent. And wasn't that some trick for a nice Chinese boy from the wilds of a Boston suburb? In contrast, he, Mark Lee, the youngest of the boys, was Mr. Real World. He had gone from a public high school to a state college and lived, being the last son, the dumb son, his father's son.

These days, Mark wore blue jeans and T-shirts and drove a red Ford station wagon with a factory third seat he had liberated from a car wreck in a junkyard. This he had installed himself, much to the delight of his kids. Mark once explained to Addie how he fig-ured the third seat had to be a feature the dealer popped in, rather than had factory-installed, and, of course, he was right. Mark was always, well, on the mark. This was how he had come to head the family building business. Mark could predict which streets would get plowed first in a snowstorm, and how long the whole cleanup would take. He could make sure their street was plowed early—not so early as to attract attention, but early. Mark was the brother who had arranged for, and possibly fixed up, the video camera, loading and charging it for immediate use.

As for the card, Addie was amazed to see that Mark and Billy had gotten Neddie, her number-one brother, to sign it himself, in that chicken-scratch handwriting that Mark used to call positive proof that Neddie was headed for a padded cell, until Neddie indeed went into the hospital. Then, for once, Mark didn't say anything at all, prompting Billy to remark how heartening it was to see that Mark sometimes knew when to shut up. Neddie himself was not physically there at the shower, but so familiar was his absence, that it had become his presence. In this, he was unlike their stepfather, Reynolds, who could be considered more authentically missing.

THE SHOWER PROPER

Now Addie panned around the room. To zoom or not to zoom? From the casbah comfort of an upholstered rocking chair, Addie tipped forward, touching her feet to the floor to steady the shot. Forward—voilà. There was her beaming husband, Rex, looking as though he had just won a Nobel Prize, the first ever given for paternity. He called himself a mongrel Mongol, and indeed had the romantic slashing brow and broad planar cheeks that evoked a windblown life chasing sheep on the steppe; never mind that he was half Japanese. Addie zoomed back. Now you could see how he was flanked by females. These were friends of Addie's, around whom Rex had looped his arms playboy-style. Actually, he was a sensitive intellectual engaged in good works, as were Addie's friends. Nevertheless, they all waved little flat babe waves before Rex disengaged and leaned forward, elbows on his knees, with a serious look. "I just want to say," he announced, "now, and for history, that you, Addie Wing, are the love of my life. My harem is nothing to me."

At this everyone laughed, even Addie's women's studies friends, who had over the years practically come to appreciate him. "That's good, since I'm sure you are nothing to them," she managed—not the best reply, but people did laugh at that, too. After all, it was her shower, and they loved her. Addie had always thought Rex should have married someone with a gift for the comeback line rather than someone who felt pressured by banter, as she did. But he claimed it was hard enough being married to someone who was always right; he at least needed to know the good lines were his.

Next in her viewfinder were her brothers Mark and Billy, the study in contrasts who nonetheless looked surprisingly alike. Mark's hair was short, Billy's in a ponytail. But both wore shorts that showed off their surpassing fitness and sparsely hairy legs. They both seemed to be idling about, awaiting suitable challenge; and they waved with similar nonchalance, as if this was yet another thing they could do one-handed.

"Try the date button," said Mark.

Billy turned toward some veggie dip.

"Billy," said Addie. "You have to say something."

He turned around, wielding a largish spear of broccoli like a microphone. "This is Billy Wing, reporting live from the shower of the century," he said. Then he turned away from the camera again.

"Come on," said Addie.

"Some party," he said.

"Billy."

"Some camera."

"Billy."

"I'm going to work for Mark," he said. "Starting tomorrow."

"What?" said Addie.

"He'll be a real asset," said Mark.

"It is my deepest ambition," intoned Billy. He wielded his broccoli mike once again. "I have always yearned to be an asset."

Beside them chattered Addie's three sisters-in-law, none of

whom knew what irony was. Mark's wife seemed to have modeled herself on the late Princess Diana; this involved overdressing and a vaguely tragic air. Then there were Addie's roommates from college and graduate school, some of whom had updated, but others of whom you could pick out in a lineup as ex-hippies. Emma Rose, for example, wore all natural fiber; Mark said she looked like a model for a burlap store. The one buddy Addie had kept up with from junior high, Jessica, likewise still did a gypsy look, with a matching manner that involved clasping people's hands as she talked. In general, though, updated or not, most people looked surprisingly happy for their age. Still young, as opposed to plain young, they no longer talked about Life as if it were the next city on a walking tour. They were knowledgeable about knee procedures and dental work, and wary of what came next—either justifiably or needlessly; Addie had heard both. For now Addie saw in her eyepiece that apprehension gave rise to a special clear happiness—magical as the blue ice skylight that let a wavery square of sun into modern-day igloos.

That happiness was broken, thankfully, by only one unhappy mother, hers. Addie swept guiltily past Madame Lee, as Rex called her, vaguely hoping that Rex had not put her on wrapping-paper duty. For even after forty years here, Regina was ambivalent at best about pitching in American-style at events like these. She took offense at the idea that anyone would expect her to help like a servant. "And asking is expecting," Addie explained to Rex, who locked eyes with her as she spoke and, in a manner he had learned in a sensitivity seminar, received her words. "I hear you," he said. "You have spoken."

Yet there was Regina, balling up the paper with the nobly suffering air of a movie star in a labor camp, while Addie's mother-in-law, on Prozac, fairly beamed with the honor of keeping a gift inventory. Doreen waved enthusiastically at the camera lest it miss her, and, when Addie zoomed in, advised for the a⟨ important. Believe me. You simply cannot rely on ⟨ nisei from Hawaii, Doreen had more foundation than the other, and had once told Addie that Japan was the most amazing place she had ever been. *The women there put on nylons to go to the grocery store,* she said. *The men get perms.*

Behind Doreen stood Addie's friend Lorna's books—beat-up seminal tomes subsumed by bright volumes of Brazelton and Leach. Nearby, world-travel artifacts commingled with a wide selection of educational toys and stuffed sea creatures—a family of orca whales, a dolphin, a manta ray—and what appeared to be a token teddy bear. In front of them stood the automatic baby swing that Lorna had said used an unconscionable number of batteries. If she had it to do over again, she would get a wind-up, but anyway, she hoped Addie would accept the loan, which she accompanied with a crateful of batteries of every size. This, in addition to the shower, was her present to Addie, who had exclaimed with real surprise when she opened it. "Everything takes batteries," said Lorna. There was another box, too, from Lorna's husband, Ken, to Rex. It was full of Scotch tape. "All will become clear in time," said Ken. "Just wait."

Addie filmed these things, thinking how glad she was that, like Neddie and Reynolds, she was not going to be in the picture. She wondered, too, whether she could have avoided gaining forty pounds with this pregnancy, and whether anyone gained twenty-five who was not under twenty-five. These thoughts were so retrograde that she could hardly believe them hers. She had read *The Second Sex* in high school, and underlined everything. All her adult life, she had refused to be objectified. Yet the thoughts seemed to have a life of their own, like her body, potent and miraculous, yet big as a submersible, and on a mission she was most notably not directing.

The baby began an aerobics routine; Addie flexed her turgid feet. People called summer pregnancies the worst, but at least you were spared having to wear real shoes. And if your body seemed a spectacle, at least everybody else was a body, too, all armpits and skin moles. She was hardly the only one with an inelegant appendage. Addie sneakily recorded for the ages several inelegant appendages, then more sweetly continued on, not only to the batteries and the Scotch tape but to the more traditional presents. These Addie made her friends hold up and explain.

"This is a wipe warmer, for to pamper your child's tush."

"This is a rattle, designed to encourage early grasping."

"This is a breast pump, for comic relief."

Inspired, it seemed, by their testimonial, Regina produced from the next room one last present. She moved slowly, as if, though the same age as Rex's mother, she were far more elderly. She had had her hair done in a petrified dandelion puff for the shower, and she put her hand up to it from time to time as if to be sure it was stage-ready.

The present was not wrapped. "I explain for you," she offered; and so Addie filmed as her mother held up a stuffed sailfish.

"This fish your stepfather give to me for last year anniversary present," she said. "This year I give to you. We are getting divorced after thirty-five years marriage. I have no place even to stay now."

At this, Addie put down the camera, leapt out of her chair—as best she could leap—and of course offered her mother sanctuary with her. She took the sailfish from Regina's arms, attempting to embrace her mother at the same time. This was not quite possible, but the intention was clear. Addie's stepbrother, Mark, picked up the camera and caught the rest of the exchange. "I am your difficult mother. Our whole lives we fight. How can I move into your house?" Still Addie insisted, trying as she spoke to put the sailfish down. Its sail was so high that she could barely see over it. She made her heartfelt offer into a shellacked ribbed fin. But it was heard. By the time a friend rescued Addie from the trophy, other friends had chimed in encouragingly.

"Perfect!" proclaimed Jessica, predictably ecstatic. After all, Addie and Rex were going to need help, and how nice for the baby to get to know its grandmother!

"No help." Regina waved her wave of flat refusal, her palm adamantly prominent. Her beautiful fingers were stiffly splayed in a no-nonsense manner; only her pinkie arched back coyly with a slight crook. (This was the same pinkie that reared like a prairie dog when she picked up a teacup.) Her manner, correspondingly, was despairing in an alert sort of way—edging, like the cry of a child, from a wail of sheer pain to something more artistic. Addie watched as the wave of flat refusal became a wave of polite refusal, then of pro forma refusal. By this time, Regina's predicament had inspired a kind of call and response.

"No help, no help," said Regina.

"Of course you'll be a help!" said the crowd.

"Addie has no room."

"Addie will make room!"

"Who wants an old lady come live with them?"

"They do, they do! They welcome you! They want you!"

Finally, Madame Lee agreed to be welcomed. The crowd burst into applause, as if on a TV show. Then Doreen moved to congratulate Regina while Lorna and Ken brought out dessert—a cake with a jogger stroller drawn on top. The jogger stroller held a big question mark.

PILLOW TALK

"Shh. See? It's moving."

Rex successfully connected with a kick but then drew Addie's

T-shirt back down like a shade and continued his miracle appreciation through the cloth. In principle, he adored her belly, her taut and mottled, veiny belly, with its popped-out navel like a gag from a joke shop. But in practice, he did not adore it. In this way, he was out of step with his times. He dimly recognized that the body had in fact snuck in, midcentury, to dominate contemporary thought. No truth but in things. No ideas but in hormones. Yet how was he supposed to feel about Addie's avid interest in their neighbor's dog's new litter, for example? A year ago, it would have been Frank Stella's midcareer crisis that elicited that kind of deeply involved reaction. The switch to the Indian Birds, and what Caravaggio would have thought of these aggressive steel constructions projecting a foot out from the wall. Now Rex watched, aghast, as Addie and the bitch exchanged soulful glances of mutual understanding. The bitch was a dachshund, no less. And what did Addie talk of now, endlessly, but her body? This twinge, that twinge, a funny fullness, a distinct soreness. Stretching, rumblings, gas. Her entire belly sometimes lurched from one side to the other as the baby sought to get more comfortable. How uncomfortable they all were! He least of all; and yet it was no small, poignant, delighted terror he felt as he watched Addie grow larger than he and sexually voracious. More, more, more. This wasn't in any manual he had read.

"My mother," she said.

He shook his head sympathetically. "We can only hope she'll come to our senses."

"Very funny. The scoop is that Reynolds's new woman lives right here in town. My mother ran into them at the club, can you imagine? A redhead wearing that kind of bikini where the top doesn't even match the bottom."

"No wonder your mother's upset."

"Where are we going to put her?"

"In the nursery, of course. Where she belongs."

"It'll be like having twins."

Rex thought this over. "There's always murder," he concluded. "Smother her with a pillow."

"Don't you think that would be ethically problematic? If we didn't even first try to discourage her from moving in?"

"We'll smother her with a pillow and see if that discourages her."

"The fish wasn't even an anniversary present. I mean, Reynolds gave it to her, but not for their anniversary."

"Did he at least catch it himself?"

Addie sighed. "I don't know why I married you," she said, closing her eyes firmly. She had an air of utter resignation. "You are truly hard to talk to." All the same, she cagily advanced a hand onto his waiting thigh.

THE PROBLEM

Their condo, on the second floor of a three-family house, was not large. Their condo was, in fact, small, as befitted two people with meaningful professions. Rex did low-income housing in the inner city, which represented a personal victory of sorts. It had been a struggle for him, the firstborn of his family, to become this variety of do-gooder. Not that there had never been a family do-gooder before. In fact, his mother's father had been a Buddhist priest in Japan. He had had his own temple, via which he had made a fortune mumbling sutras at funerals.

The trouble was that Doreen thought Rex should find himself a similar monopoly situation. For example, as a doctor in some remote area. He could open his own clinic, et cetera. Rex had explained, explained, and finally given up explaining. Finally he had turned *deaf ear*, as Doreen complained—an achievement, to his mind, in itself. He had felt sorry for his classmates with better hearing who had gone to medical school. The ones with immigrant parents in particular seemed to do nothing but perform, perform, only to be pronounced still lacking. If they were practitioners, they weren't researchers. If they were internists, they weren't surgeons. Rex had realized that you had to live your own life. He had broken with his family's expectations—realizing, as he liked to admit, that he could use all the nobility he could get.

But more recently, he noticed that, parent-plagued or not, his doctor friends were certainly most comfortably trapped. How easy it was to get burned on second houses, they lamented. Whereas, what with the baby coming, he was beginning to wonder whether he couldn't trade in, say, half of his unimpeachable integrity for cash. This was to keep from qualifying to live in one of his housing projects himself.

In this regard, Addie, a garden designer, was no help. If she would go back to school, she might at least someday charge landscape architect rates. But she pointedly did not because, she said, she liked the humbleness of her work as it was. In her twenties, she had aspired to achieve immortality as a sculptress; she had even had a flirtation with marble. But in her thirties, she had come to realize that all her ambition was about death. It was about defying death. It was about denying death. It was about death, death, death! A friend had given her a book about this; the friend later asked for the book back. But it was too late. Addie was working then in primitive materials like soap and felt, and achieving some recognition for her work. She had, in fact, just had a piece of hers hung at the Museum of Fine Arts right opposite a Lucian Freud when she realized that art was over for her.

That's when she became, first a hospice worker, and then an artisan—a person who took small spaces and simply made them beautiful. Sometimes her efforts were nontraditional. Once she made a pergola of Coke bottles; once a mossy swale; once a garden of tennis balls on stakes. But she also planted tree hydrangeas for children to run under, coneflowers to attract butterflies. She did reliable, joyous gardens for Rex's city projects. Everything was addressed to the humans living in the shadow of the large mountain, and not to the mountain itself.

ADDIE'S ROOM BECOMES REGINA'S ROOM

It wasn't until Regina and the baby that Addie wished her practice a less modest activity. For as the site of a modest activity, Addie's workroom became an irresistible topic of discussion.

"I don't know how comfortable I am, your books and paper everywhere," said Regina. "Where am I going to put my clothes?"

Regina said, "Once the baby comes, you will have no time for gardening anyway."

" 'Gardening,' she called it," grumbled Addie to Rex.

Luckily, Mark, hearing of their dilemma, offered to help. "We'll convert that kitchen closet of yours into a home office," he said. "Put in a pull-down desk with some built-in storage. I've got some exotic wood trim from another job—you can have it for free. And Billy of the Northlands can supply the labor. It's his chance to learn how to hold a hammer. I'll charge you cost."

Rex and Addie pondered this offer. Would it simply encourage Regina never to move out?

"Of course Mark wants her to be comfortable here," said Rex. "He's afraid she'll be looking next at his beautiful place, with the renovated kitchen and the pool in the backyard. He knows if she could stand his wife, he'd be sunk."

"Billy says she made all that up about Bloomingdale's," said Addie.

"How interesting," said Rex.

"I can't work in a closet," said Addie.

Addie said, "The kitchen is noisy."

All the same, the next Saturday they were looking at plans, with Mark, in the kitchen, when the first of the contractions came. Was it a Braxton-Hicks? thought Addie. But it was nothing like a Braxton-Hicks.

"It's happening," said Addie. She stood up. She sat back down.

"What's happening?" said Rex, looking at the drawings. Rex loved drawings.

"Nothing," she said then, and leaned over the drawings, too, as if deliriously absorbed. Meanwhile, Mark took his shoes off. Mark made himself a cup of coffee. Mark helped himself to a bagel, and to the lox that had been meant for three. Once upon a time, Neddie the Absent used to look around at them all and announce, *You see me not,* to which Regina would reply, *What you talking about?* and *You must be crazy!* Now Addie was going to a hospital, too. For a different reason, thankfully; and how much more likely it was that she would have too many visitors than too few. Yet as Mark talked of a board that could be easily unhinged, she thought of Neddie, and of Billy, and of their father, so long dead she had no memory of him. Had Neddie ever held a newborn before? Probably not, she guessed. Another contraction gripped her; she looked at the clock, her mind turning, fearfully, toward labor. But even as it turned, she thought for just one more moment of what a treat it would be for Neddie to meet the baby. She could picture his face already, soft with delight, yet crying—he cried at everything, poor Neddie. She could picture him trembling like an old man at the very prospect of visitors. *This is my child,* she would say. He would say, *But of course.* Then he would open his arms with the sudden strength of the happy. *How very bald,* he would say. *How very red.* And, *How nice to have a new stranger in the family.*

CHIN

I wasn't his friend, but I wasn't one of the main kids who hounded him up onto the shed roof, either. Sure I'd lob a rock or two, but this was our stage of life back then, someplace between the arm and the fist. Not to chuck nothing would have been against nature, and I never did him one he couldn't duck easy, especially being as fast as he was—basically the fastest kid in the ninth grade, and one of the smartest besides, smarter even than yours truly, the official class underachiever. I tested so high on my IQ that the school psychologists made me take the test over, nobody could believe it. They've been hounding me to apply myself ever since. But Chin was smart, too—not so much in math and science as in stuff like history and English. How's that for irony? And he was a good climber, you had to give him that, the only kid who could scale that shed wall, period. Because that wall didn't have no handholds or footholds. In fact, the naked eye would've pronounced that wall plain concrete; you had to wonder if the kid had some kind of special vision, so that he could look at that wall and see a way up. Maybe where we saw wall, he saw cracks, or maybe there was something he knew in his body about walls; or maybe they didn't have walls in China, besides the Great Wall, that is, so that he knew a wall was only a wall because we thought it was a wall. That might be getting philosophical. But you know, I've seen guys do that in basketball, find the basket in ways you can't account for. You can rewind the tape and watch the replay until your eyeballs pop, but finally you've got to say that obstacles are not always obstacles for these guys. Things melt away for them.

Gus said it was on account of there was monkey feet inside his sneakers that the kid could get up there. That was the day the kid started stockpiling the rocks we threw and raining them back down on us. A fall day, full of the crack and smell of people burning leaves illegally. It was just like the monkeys in the zoo when they get mad at the zookeepers, that's what I said. I saw that on TV once. But Gus blew a smoke ring and considered it like a sunset, then said even though you couldn't see the kid's monkey feet, they were like hands and could grip onto things. He said you've never seen such long toes, or such weird toenails, either, and that the toenails were these little bitty slits, like his eyes. And that, he said, was why he was going to drown me in a douche bag if I threw any more rocks without paying attention. He said I was fucking arming the ape.

We didn't live in the same building, that kid and me. His name was Chin or something, like chin-up we used to say, and his family lived in the garden apartment next door to ours. This was in scenic Yonkers, New York, home of Central Avenue. We were both stuck on the ground floor, where everyone could look right into your kitchen. It was like having people look up your dress, my ma said, and they were smack across the alley from us. So you see, if I'd really wanted to nail him with a rock, I could've done it anytime their windows were open if I didn't want to break any glass. And I could've done it any time at all if I didn't care about noise and commotion and getting a JD card like the Beyer kid got for climbing the water tower. Of course, they didn't open their windows much, the Chins. My ma said it was because they were Chinese people—you know, like Chinese food, from China, she said, and then she cuffed me for playing dumb and getting her to explain what a Chinese was when they were getting to be a fact of life. Not like in California or Queens, but they were definitely proliferating, along with a lot of other people who could tell you where they came from, if they spoke English. They weren't like us who came from Yonkers and didn't have no special foods, unless you wanted to count fries. Gus never could see why we couldn't count fries. My own hunch, though, guess why, was that they just might be French. Not that I said so. I was more interested in why everybody suddenly had to have a special food. And why was everybody asking what your family was? First time somebody asked me that, I had no idea what they were talking about. But after a while, I said, Vanilla. I said that because I didn't want to say we were nothing, my family was nothing.

My ma said that the Chins kept their windows shut because they liked their apartment hot, seeing as how it was what they were used to. People keep to what they're used to, she liked to say, though she also liked to say, Wait and see, you know your taste changes. Especially to my big sister she was always saying that, because my sis was getting married for real this time, to this hairdresser who had suddenly started offering her free bang trims anytime. Out of the blue, this was. He was a thinker, this Ray. He had it all figured out, how from doing the bang trim he could get to talking about her beautiful blue eyes. And damned if he wasn't right that a lot of people, including yours truly, had never particularly noticed her eyes, what with the hair hanging in them. A real truth-teller, that Ray was, and sharp as a narc. It was all that practice with women all day long, my ma said. He knows how to make a woman feel like a queen, not like your pa, who knows how to make her feel like shit. She was as excited as my sis, that's the truth, now that this Ray and her Debi were hitting the aisle sure enough. Ray was doing my ma's hair free, too, every other day just about, trying to fine-tune her do for the wedding, and in between she was trying to pitch a couple of last You knows across to Debi while she could. Kind of a cram course.

But my pa said the Chins did that with their windows because somebody put a cherry bomb in their kitchen for fun one day, and it upset them. Maybe they didn't know it was just a cherry bomb. Who knows what they thought it was, but they beat up Chin over it; that much we did know, because we could see everything and hear everything they did over there, especially if we turned the TV down, which we sometimes did for a fight. If only more was in English, we could've understood everything, too. Instead all we caught was that Chin got beat up over the cherry bomb, as if they thought it was owing to him that somebody put the bomb in the window. Go figure.

Chin got beat up a lot—this wasn't the first time. He got beat up on account of he played hooky from school sometimes, and he got beat up on account of he mouthed off to his pa, and he got beat up on account of he once got a C in math, which was why right near the bomb site there was a blackboard in the kitchen. Nights he wasn't getting beaten up, he was parked in front of the blackboard doing equations with his pa, who people said was not satisfied with Chin plain getting the correct answer in algebra, he had to be able to get it two or three ways. Also he got beat up because he liked to find little presents for himself and his sis and his ma. He did this in stores without paying for them, and that pissed the hell out of his pa. On principle, people said, but maybe he just felt left out. I always thought Chin should've known enough to get something for his pa, too.

But really Chin got beat up, my pa said, because Mr. Chin had this weird cheek. He had some kind of infection in some kind of hole, and as a result, the cheek shook and for a long time he wouldn't go to the doctor, seeing as how in China he used to be a doctor himself. Here he was a cab driver—the worst driver in the city, we're talking someone who would sooner puke on the Pope than cut across two lanes of traffic. He had a little plastic sleeve on the passenger-side visor where he displayed his driver's license; that's how much it meant to him that he'd actually gotten one. But in China he'd been a doctor, and as a result, he refused to go to a doctor here until his whole cheek was about gone. Thought he should be able to cure himself with herbs. Now even with the missus out working down at the dry cleaners, they were getting cleaned out themselves, what with the bills. They're going to need that boy for their old age, that's what my pa said. Cabbies don't have no pension plan like firemen and policemen and everybody else. They can't afford for him to go wrong, he's going to have to step up to the plate and hit that ball into the bleachers for them. That's why he gets beat, so he'll grow up to be a doctor who can practice in America. They want that kid to have his M.D. hanging up instead of his driver's license.

That was our general theory of why Chin got the treatment. But this time was maybe different. This time my pa wondered if maybe Chin's pa thought he was in some kind of a gang. He asked me if Chin was or wasn't, and I said no way was he in anything. Nobody hung with Chin, why would anybody hang with the guy everyone wanted to break? Unless you wanted them to try and break you, too. That's when my pa nodded in that captain of the force way you see on TV, and I was glad I told him. It made me feel like I'd forked over valuable information to the guy who ought to know. I felt like I could relax after I'd told him, even though maybe it was Mr. Chin who really should've known. Who knows but maybe my pa should've told Mr. Chin. Though what was he going to do, call him up and say, This is our theory next door? The truth is, I understood my pa. Like maybe I should've told Gus that Chin didn't actually have monkey feet, because I've seen his feet top and bottom through my pa's binoculars, and they were just regular. But let's face it, people don't want to be told much. And what difference did it make that I didn't think his toes were even that long, or that I could see them completely plain because his pa used to make him kneel when he wanted to beat him? What difference does it make what anybody's seen? Sometimes I think I should've kept my eyes on the TV where they belonged, instead of watching stuff I couldn't turn off. Chin's pa used to use a belt mostly, but sometimes he used a metal garden stake, and with every single whack, I used to think how glad I was that it was Chin and not me that had those big welts rising up out of his back skin. They looked like some great special effect, these oozy red caterpillars crawling over some older pinkish ones. Chin never moved or said anything, and that just infuriated his pa more. You could see it so clear, you almost felt sorry for him. Here he had this garden stake and there was nothing he could do. What with his cheek all wrapped up, he had to stop the beating every now and then to readjust his bandage.

My pa used a ruler on me once, just like the one they used at school—Big Bertha, we called it, a solid eighteen inches, and if you flinched, you got hit another three times on the hands. Naturally, Chin never did, as a result of the advanced training he got at home. People said he didn't feel nothing; he was like a horse you had to kick with heel spurs, your plain heel just tickled. But I wasn't used to torture instruments. We didn't believe in that sort of thing in my house. Even that time my pa did get out the ruler, it broke and he had to go back to using his hand. That was bad enough. My pa was a fireman, meaning he was a lot stronger than Chin's pa was ever going to be, which maybe had nothing to do with anything. But my theory was, it was on account of that he knew he wasn't that strong that Mr. Chin used the garden stake on Chin, and once on the sister, too.

She wasn't as old as my sister, and she wasn't that pretty, and she wasn't that smart, and you were just glad when you looked at her that you weren't her gym teacher. She wore these glasses that looked like they were designed to fall off, and she moseyed down the school halls the way her pa did the highway—keeping all the way to the right and hesitating dangerously in the intersections. But she had a beautiful voice and was always doing the solo at school assembly. Some boring thing—the songs at school were all worse than ever since Mr. Reardon, the math teacher, had to take over music. He was so musical, people had to show him how to work those black stands; he didn't know you could adjust them, he thought they came in sizes. To be fair, he asked three times if he couldn't do study hall instead. But Chin's sister managed to wring something out of the songs he picked somehow. Everything she sang sounded like her. It was funny—she never talked, this girl, and everybody called her quiet, but when she sang, she filled up the whole auditorium and you completely forgot she wore these glasses people said were bulletproof.

It wasn't the usual thing that the sister got hit. But one day she threatened to move out of the house, actually stomped out into the snow, saying that she could not stand to watch what was going on anymore. Then her pa hauled her back and beat her, too. At least he left her clothes on and didn't make her kneel. She got to stand and only fell on the floor, curled up, by choice. But here was the sad thing: It turned out you could hear her singing voice when she cried; she still sounded like herself. She didn't look like herself with her glasses off, though, and nobody else did, either. Chin the unflinching turned so red in the face, he looked as though blood beads were going to come busting straight out of his pores, and he started pounding the wall so hard, he put craters in it. His ma told him to stop, but he kept going, until finally she packed a suitcase and put the sister's glasses back on for her. Ma Chin had to tape the suitcase with duct tape to get it to stay shut. Then Ma Chin and the sister both put on their coats and headed for the front door. The snowflakes by then were so giant, you'd think there was a closeout sale on underwear going on up in heaven. Still the dynamic duo marched out into the neighborhood and up our little hill without any boots. Right up the middle of the street, they went; I guess there being two of them bucked up the sister. Ma Chin started out with the suitcase, but by the time they'd reached the hill, the sister'd wrestled it away from her. Another unexpected physical feat. It was cold out, and so dark that what with all the snow, the light from the streetlights appeared to be falling down too, and kind of drifting around. My pa wondered out loud if he should give our neighbors a friendly lift someplace. After all, the Chins had no car, and it was a long walk over to the bus stop. But what would he say? Excuse me, I just happened to be out driving?

He was trying to work this out with my ma, but she had to tell him first how Ray would know what to say without having to consult nobody and how glad she was that her Debi wasn't marrying nobody like him. Ray, Ray, Ray! my pa said finally. Why don't you go fuck him yourself instead of using your daughter? Then he sat right in the kitchen window, where anybody who bothered to look could see him, and watched as Ma Chin and the sister stopped and had themselves a little conference. They were up to their ankles in snow, neither in one streetlight cone or the next, but smack in between. They jawed for a long time. Then they moved a little farther up the incline and stopped and jawed again, sheltering their glasses from the snow with their hands. They almost looked like lifeguards out there, trying to keep the sun out of their eyes, except that they didn't seem to know that they were supposed to be looking for something. Probably their glasses were all fogged up. Still my pa watched them and watched them while I had a look at Chin and his pa back at the ranch, and saw the most astounding thing of all: They were back at the blackboard, working problems out. Mr. Chin had a cup of tea made, and you couldn't see his face on account of his bandage, but he was gesturing with the eraser and Chin was nodding. How do you figure? I half-wanted to say something to my pa, to point out this useless fact. But my pa was too busy sitting in the window with the lights on, waiting for the Chin women to shout Fire! or something, I guess. He wanted them to behold him there, all lit up, their rescuer. Unfortunately, though, it was snowing out, not burning, and their heads were bent and their eyes were on the ground as they dragged their broken suitcase straight back across our view.

IN THE AMERICAN SOCIETY

HIS OWN SOCIETY

When my father took over the pancake house, it was to send my little sister, Mona, and me to college. We were only in junior high at the time, but my father believed in getting a jump on things. "Those Americans always saying it," he told us. "Smart guys thinking in advance." My mother elaborated, explaining that businesses took bringing up, like children. They could take years to get going, she said, years.

In this case, though, we got rich right away. At two months, we were breaking even, and at four, those same hotcakes that could barely withstand the weight of butter and syrup were supporting our family with ease. My mother bought a station wagon with air conditioning, my father an oversized red vinyl recliner for the back room; and as time went on and the business continued to thrive, my father started to talk about his grandfather, and the village he had reigned over in China—things my father had never talked about when he worked for other people. He told us about the bags of rice his family would give out to the poor at New Year's, and about the people who came to beg, on their hands and knees, for his grandfather to intercede for the more wayward of their relatives. "Like that Godfather in the movie," he would tell us as, feet up, he distributed paychecks. Sometimes an employee would get two green envelopes instead of one, which meant that Jimmy needed a tooth pulled, say, or that Tiffany's husband was in the clinker again. "It's nothing, nothing," he would insist, sinking back into his chair. "Who else is going to taking care of you people?"

My mother would mostly just sigh about it. "Your father thinks this is China," she would say, and then she would go back to her mending. Once in a while, though, when my father had given away a particularly large sum, she would exclaim, outraged, "But this here is the *U—S—of—A!*"—this apparently having been what she used to tell immigrant stock boys when they came in late.

She didn't work at the supermarket anymore; but she had made it to the rank of manager before she left, and this had given her not only new words and phrases but new ideas about herself, and about America, and about what was what in general. She had opinions about how downtown should be zoned; she could pump her own gas and check her own oil; and for all that she used to chide Mona and me for being copycats, she herself was now interested in espadrilles, and wallpaper, and, most recently, the town country club.

"So join already," said Mona, flicking a fly off her knee.

My mother enumerated the problems as she sliced up a quarter round of watermelon. There was the cost. There was the waiting list. There was the fact that no one in our family played either tennis or golf.

"So what?" said Mona.

"It would be waste," said my mother.

"Me and Callie can swim in the pool."

"Anyway, you need that recommendation letter from a member."

"Come *on*," said Mona. "Annie's mom'd write you a letter in a *sec*."

My mother's knife glinted in the early-summer sun. I spread some more newspaper on the picnic table.

"Plus, you have to eat there twice a month. You know what that means." My mother cut another, enormous slice of fruit.

"No, I *don't* know what that means," said Mona.

"It means Dad would have to wear a jacket, dummy," I said.

"Oh! Oh! Oh!" said Mona, clasping her hand to her breast. "Oh! Oh! Oh! Oh! Oh!"

We all laughed: My father had no use for nice clothes, and would wear only ten-year-old shirts, with grease-spotted pants, to show how little he cared what anyone thought.

"Your father doesn't believe in joining the American society," said my mother. "He wants to have his own society."

"So go to dinner without him." Mona shot her seeds out in long arcs over the lawn. "Who cares what he thinks?"

But of course, we all did care, and knew my mother could not simply up and do as she pleased. For to embrace what my father embraced was to love him; and to embrace something else was to betray him.

He demanded a similar sort of loyalty of his workers, whom he treated more like servants than employees. Not in the beginning, of course. In the beginning, all he wanted was for them to keep on doing what they used to do, to which end he concentrated mostly on leaving them alone. As the months passed, though, he expected more and more of them, with the result that, for all his largesse, he began to have trouble keeping help. The cooks and busboys complained that he asked them to fix radiators and trim hedges, not only at the restaurant but at our house; the waitresses, that he sent them on errands, and made them chauffeur him around. Our headwaitress, Gertrude, claimed that he once even asked her to scratch his back.

"It's not just the blacks don't believe in slavery," she said when she quit.

My father never quite registered her complaints, though, nor those of the others who left. Even after Eleanor quit, then Tiffany, and Gerald, and Jimmy, and even his best cook, Eureka Andy, for whom he had bought new glasses, he remained mostly convinced that the fault lay with them.

"All they understand is that assemble line," he lamented. "Robots, they are. They want to be robots."

There were occasions when the clear running truth seemed to eddy, when he would pinch the vinyl of his chair up into little peaks and wonder if he was doing things right. But with time he would always smooth the peaks back down; and when business started to slide in the spring, he kept on like a horse in his ways.

By the summer, our dish boy was overwhelmed with scraping. It was no longer just the hash browns that people were leaving for trash, and the service was as bad as the food. The waitresses served up French pancakes instead of German, apple juice instead of orange. They spilled things on laps, on coats. On the Fourth of July, some greenhorn sent an entire side of fries slaloming down a lady's *Massif Central*. Meanwhile, in the back room, my father labored through articles on the economy.

"What is housing starts?" he puzzled. "What is GNP?"

Mona and I did what we could, filling in as busgirls and dish-washers, and, one afternoon, stuffing the comments box by the cashier's desk. That was Mona's idea. We rustled up a variety of pens and pencils, checked boxes for an hour, smeared the cards with coffee and grease, and waited. It took a few days for my father to notice that the box was full, and he didn't say anything about it for a few days more. Finally, though, he started to complain of fatigue; and then he began to complain that the staff was not what it could be. We encouraged him in this—pointing out, for instance, how many dishes got chipped. But in the end all that happened was that, for the first time since we took over the restaurant, my father got it into his head to fire someone. Skip, a skinny busboy who was saving up for a sports car, said nothing as my father mumbled on about the price of dishes. My father's hands shook as he wrote out the severance check; and once it was over, he spent the rest of the day napping in his chair.

Since it was going on midsummer, Skip wasn't easy to replace. We hung a sign in the window and advertised in the paper, but no one called the first week, and the person who called the second didn't show up for his interview. The third week, my father phoned Skip to see if he would come back, but a friend of his had already sold him a Corvette for cheap.

Finally, a Chinese guy named Booker turned up. He couldn't have been more than thirty, and was wearing a lighthearted seersucker suit, but he looked as though life had him pinned. His eyes were bloodshot and his chest sunken, and the muscles of his neck seemed to strain with the effort of holding his head up. In a single dry breath he told us that he had never bused tables but was willing to learn, and that he was on the lam from the deportation authorities.

"I do not want to lie to you," he kept saying. He had come to the United States on a student visa but had run out of money and was now in a bind. He was loath to go back to Taiwan, as it happened—he looked up at this point, to be sure my father wasn't pro-KMT—but all he had was a phony Social Security card, and a willingness to absorb all blame, should anything untoward come to pass.

"I do not think, anyway, that it is against law to hire me, only to be me," he said, smiling faintly.

Anyone else would have examined him on this, but my father conceived of laws as speed bumps rather than curbs. He wiped the counter with his sleeve, and told Booker to report the next morning.

"I will be good worker," said Booker.

"Good," said my father.

"Anything you want me to do, I will do."

My father nodded.

Booker seemed to sink into himself for a moment. "Thank you," he said finally. "I am appreciate your help. I am very, very appreciate for everything."

My father looked at him. "Did you eat today?" he asked in Mandarin.

Booker pulled at the hem of his jacket.

"Sit down," said my father. "Please, have a seat."

My father didn't tell my mother about Booker, and my mother didn't tell my father about the country club. She would never have applied, except that Mona, while over at Annie's, had let it drop that our mother wanted to join. Mrs. Lardner came by the very next day.

"Why, I'd be honored and delighted to write you people a letter," she said. Her skirt billowed around her.

"Thank you so much," said my mother. "But it's too much trouble for you, and also my husband is . . ."

"Oh, it's no trouble at all, no trouble at all. I tell you." She leaned forward, so that her chest freckles showed. "I know just how it is. It's a secret of course, but, you know, my natural father was Jewish. Can you see it? Just look at my skin."

"My husband," said my mother.

"I'd be honored and delighted," said Mrs. Lardner, with a little wave of her hands. "Just honored and delighted."

Mona was triumphant. "See, Mom," she said, waltzing around the kitchen when Mrs. Lardner left. "What did I tell you? 'I'm honored and delighted, just honored and delighted.' " She waved her hands in the air.

"You know, the Chinese have a saying," said my mother. "To do nothing is better than to overdo. You mean well, but you tell me now what will happen."

"I'll talk Dad into it," said Mona, still waltzing. "Or I bet Callie can. He'll do anything Callie says."

"I can try, anyway," I said.

"Did you hear what I said?" said my mother. Mona bumped into the broom closet door. "You're not going to talk anything. You've already made enough trouble." She started on the dishes with a clatter.

Mona poked diffidently at a mop.

I sponged off the counter. "Anyway," I ventured. "I bet our name'll never even come up."

"That's if we're lucky," said my mother.

"There's all these people waiting," I said.

"Good." She started on a pot.

I looked over at Mona, who was still cowering in the broom closet. "In fact, there's some black family's been waiting so long, they're going to sue," I said.

My mother turned off the water. "Where'd you hear that?"

"Patty told me."

She turned the water back on, started to wash a dish, then put it down and shut the faucet.

"I'm sorry," said Mona.

"Forget it," said my mother. "Just forget it."

Booker turned out to be a model worker, whose boundless gratitude translated into a willingness to do anything. As he also learned quickly, he soon knew not only how to bus but how to cook, and how to wait tables, and how to keep the books. He fixed the walk-in door so that it stayed shut, reupholstered the torn seats in the dining room, and devised a system for tracking inventory. The only stone in the rice was that he tended to be sickly; but, reliable even in illness, he would always send a friend to take his place. In this way, we got to know Ronald, Lynn, Dirk, and Cedric, all of whom, like Booker, had problems with their legal status, and were anxious to please. They weren't all as capable as Booker, though, with the exception of Cedric, whom my father often hired even when Booker was well. A round wag of a man who called Mona and me *shou hou*—skinny monkeys—he was a professed nonsmoker who was nevertheless always begging drags off other people's cigarettes. This last habit drove our head cook, Fernando, crazy, especially since, when refused a hit, Cedric would occasionally snitch one. Winking impishly at Mona and me, he would steal up to an ashtray, take a quick puff, and then break out laughing, so that the smoke came rolling out of his mouth in a great incriminatory cloud. Fernando accused him of stealing fresh cigarettes, too, even whole packs.

"Why else do you think he's weaseling around in the back of the store all the time?" he said. His face was blotchy with anger. "The man is a frigging thief."

Other members of the staff supported him in this contention, and joined in on an "Operation Identification," which involved numbering and initialing their cigarettes—even though what they seemed to fear for wasn't so much their cigarettes as their jobs. Then one of the cooks quit; and, rather than promote someone, my father hired Cedric for the position. Rumor had it that Cedric was taking only half the normal salary; that Alex had been pressured to resign; and that my father was looking for a position with which to placate Booker, who had been bypassed because of his health.

The result was that Fernando categorically refused to work with Cedric.

"The only way I'll cook with that piece of slime," he said, shaking his huge, tattooed fist, "is if it's his ass frying on the grill."

My father cajoled and cajoled, but in the end was simply forced to put them on different schedules.

The next week, Fernando got caught stealing a carton of minute steaks. My father would not tell even Mona and me how he knew to be standing by the back door when Fernando was on his way out, but everyone suspected Booker. Everyone but Fernando, that is, who was sure Cedric had been the tip-off. My father held a staff meeting, in which he tried to reassure everyone that Alex had left on his own, and that he had no intention of firing anyone. But though he was careful not to mention Fernando, everyone was so amazed that he was being allowed to stay that Fernando was incensed nonetheless.

"Don't you all be putting your bug eyes on me," he said. "*He's* the frigging crook." He grabbed Cedric by the collar.

Cedric raised an eyebrow. "Cook, you mean," he said.

At this, Fernando punched Cedric in the mouth; and, the words he had just uttered notwithstanding, my father fired Fernando on the spot.

With everything that was happening, Mona and I were ready to be finishing up at the restaurant. It was almost time: The days were still stuffy with summer, but our window shade had started flapping in the evening as if gearing up to go out. That year, the breezes were full of salt, as they sometimes were when they came in from the east, and they blew anchors and docks through my mind like so many tumbleweeds, filling my dreams with wherries and lobsters and grainy-faced men who squinted, day in and day out, at the sky.

It was time for a change—you could feel it—and yet the pancake house was the same as ever. The day before school started, my father came home with bad news.

"Fernando called police," he said, wiping his hand on his pant leg.

My mother naturally wanted to know what police; and so, with much coughing and hawing, the long story began, the latest installment of which had the police calling Immigration, and Immigration sending an investigator. My mother sat stiff as whalebone as my father described how the man had summarily refused lunch on the house, and how my father had admitted, under pressure, that he knew there were "things" about his workers.

"So now what happens?"

My father didn't know. "Booker and Cedric went with him to the jail," he said. "But me, here I am." He laughed uncomfortably.

The next day, my father posted bail for "his boys," and waited apprehensively for something to happen. The day after that, he waited again, and the day after that, he called our neighbor's law student son, who suggested my father call the Immigration Department under an alias. My father took his advice; and it was thus that he discovered that Booker was right. It was illegal for aliens to work, but it wasn't to hire them.

In the happy interval that ensued, my father apologized to my mother, who in turn confessed about the country club, for which my father had no choice but to forgive her. Then he turned his attention back to "his boys."

My mother didn't see that there was anything to do.

"I like to talking to the judge," said my father.

"This is not China," said my mother.

"I'm only talking to him. I'm not give him money unless he wants it."

"You're going to land up in jail."

"So what else I should do?" My father threw up his hands. "Those are my boys."

"Your boys!" exploded my mother. "What about your family? What about your wife?"

My father took a long sip of tea. "You know," he said finally, "in the war my father sent our cook to the soldiers to use. He always said it—the province comes before the town, the town comes before the family."

"A restaurant is not a town," said my mother.

My father sipped at his tea again. "You know, when I first come to the United States, I also had to hide-and-seek with those deportation guys. If people did not helping me, I am not here today."

My mother scrutinized her hem.

After a minute, I volunteered that before seeing a judge, he might try a lawyer.

He turned. "Since when did you become so afraid like your mother?"

I started to say that it wasn't a matter of fear, but he cut me off. "What I need today," he said, "is a son."

My father and I spent the better part of the next day standing on lines at the Immigration office. He did not get to speak to a judge, but with much persistence he managed to speak to a special clerk, who tried to persuade him that it was not her place to extend him advice. My father, though, shamelessly plied her with compliments and offers of free pancakes, until she finally conceded that she personally doubted anything would happen to either Cedric or Booker.

"Especially if they're 'needed workers,' " she said, rubbing at the red marks her glasses left on her nose. She yawned. "Have you thought about sponsoring them to become permanent residents?"

Could he do that? My father was overjoyed. And what if he saw to it right away? Would she perhaps put in a good word with the judge?

She yawned again, her nostrils flaring. "Don't worry," she said. "They'll get a fair hearing."

My father returned jubilant. Booker and Cedric hailed him as their savior. He was like a father to them, they said; and, laughing and clapping, they made him tell the story over and over, sorting through the details like jewels. And how old was the assistant judge? And what did she say?

That evening, my father tipped the paperboy a dollar and bought a pot of mums for my mother, who suffered them to be placed on the dining room table. The next night, he took us all out to dinner. Then on Saturday, Mona found a letter and some money in an envelope on my father's chair at the restaurant.

Dear Mr. Chang,
You are the grat boss. But, we do not like to trial, so will run-
ing away now. Plese to excus us. People saying the law in
America is fears like dragon. Here is only $140. We hope some
day we can pay back the rest bale. You will getting intrest, as
you diserving, so grat a boss you are. Thank you for every
thing. In next life you will be burn in rich family, with no
more pancaks.

Yours truley,
Booker + Cedric

In the weeks that followed, my father went to the pancake house for crises, but otherwise hung around our house, fiddling idly with the sump pump and boiler in an effort, he said, to get ready for winter. It was as though he had gone into retirement, except that instead of moving south, he had moved to the basement. He even took to showering my mother with little attentions, and to calling her "old girl," and when we finally heard that the club had entertained all the applications it could for the year, he was so sympathetic that he seemed more disappointed than my mother.

IN THE AMERICAN SOCIETY

Mrs. Lardner tempered the bad news with an invitation to a bon voyage bash she was throwing for her friend Jeremy Brothers, who was going to Greece for six months.

"Do come," she urged. "You'll meet everyone, and then, you know, if things open up in the spring . . ." She waved her hands.

My mother wondered if it would be appropriate to show up at a party for someone they didn't know, but "the honest truth" was that this was an annual affair. "If it's not Greece, it's Italy," sighed Mrs. Lardner. "We really just do it because his wife left him and his daughter doesn't speak to him, and poor Jeremy just feels so *unloved.*"

She also invited Mona and me to the goings-on, to keep Annie out of the champagne. I wasn't too keen on the idea, but before I could say anything, she had already thanked us for so generously agreeing to honor her with our presence.

"A pair of little princesses, you are!" she told us. "A pair of princesses!"

The party was that Sunday. On Saturday, my mother took my father out shopping for a suit. Since it was the end of September, she insisted that he buy a worsted rather than a seersucker, even though it was only 10, rather than 50, percent off. My father protested that the weather was as hot as ever, which was true—a thick Indian summer had cozied murderously up to us—but to no avail. Summer clothes, said my mother, were not properly worn after Labor Day.

The suit was unfortunately as extravagant in length as it was in price, which posed an additional quandary, since the tailor wouldn't be in until Monday. The salesgirl, though, found a way of tacking it up temporarily.

"Maybe this suit not fit me," fretted my father.

"Just don't take your jacket off," said the salesgirl.

He gave her a tip before they left, but when he got home, he refused to remove the price tag.

"I like to asking the tailor about the size," he insisted.

"You mean you're going to *wear* it and then *return* it?" Mona rolled her eyes.

"I didn't say I'm return it," said my father stiffly. "I like to asking the tailor, that's all."

The party started off swimmingly, except that most people were wearing Bermudas or wrap skirts. Still, my parents carried on, sharing with great feeling the complaints about the heat. Of course, my father tried to eat a cracker full of shallots, and burned himself in an attempt to help Mr. Lardner turn the coals of the barbecue; but on the whole, he seemed to be doing all right. Not nearly so well as my mother, though, who had accepted an entire cupful of Mrs. Lardner's magic punch and indeed seemed to be under some spell. As Mona and Annie skirmished over whether some boy in their class inhaled when he smoked, I watched my mother take off her shoes, laughing and laughing as a man with a beard regaled her with navy stories by the pool. Apparently he had been stationed in the Orient and remembered a few words of Chinese, which made my mother laugh still more. My father excused himself to go to the bathroom, then drifted back and weighed anchor at the hors d'oeuvres table, while my mother sailed on to a group of women, who tinkled at length over the clarity of her complexion. I dug out a book I had brought.

Just when I'd cracked the spine, though, Mrs. Lardner came by to bewail her shortage of servers. Her caterers were criminals, I agreed; and the next thing I knew, I was handing out bits of marine life as amiably as I could.

"Here you go, Dad," I said, when I got to the hors d'oeuvres table.

"Everything is fine," he said.

I hesitated to leave him alone; but then the man with the beard zeroed in on him, and though he talked of nothing but my mother, I thought it would be okay to get back to work. Just at that moment, though, Jeremy Brothers lurched our way, an empty, albeit corked, wine bottle in hand. He was a slim, well-proportioned man, with a Roman nose and small eyes and a nice manly jaw that he allowed to hang agape.

"Hello," he said drunkenly. "Pleased to meet you."

"Pleased to meeting you," said my father.

"Right," said Jeremy. "Right. Listen. I have this bottle here, this most recalcitrant bottle. You see that it refuses to do my bidding. I bid it open sesame, please, and it does nothing." He pulled the cork out with his teeth, then turned the bottle upside down.

My father nodded.

"Would you have a word with it, please?" said Jeremy. The man with the beard excused himself. "Would you please have a god-damned word with it?"

My father laughed uncomfortably.

"Ah!" Jeremy bowed a little. "Excuse me, excuse me, excuse me. You are not my man, not my man at all." He bowed again and started to leave, but then circled back. "Viticulture is not your forte. Yes, I can see that, see that plainly. But may I trouble you on another matter? Forget the damned bottle." He threw it into the pool, winking at the people he splashed. "I have another matter. Do you speak Chinese?"

My father said he did not, but Jeremy pulled out a handkerchief with some characters on it anyway, saying that his daughter had sent it from Hong Kong and that he thought the characters might be some secret message.

"Long life," said my father.

"But you haven't looked at it yet."

"I know what it says without looking." My father winked at me.

"You do?"

"Yes, I do."

"You're making fun of me, aren't you?"

"No, no, no," said my father, winking again.

"Who are you anyway?" said Jeremy.

His smile fading, my father shrugged.

"Who are you?"

My father shrugged again.

Jeremy began to roar. "This is my party, *my party,* and I've never seen you before in my life." My father backed up as Jeremy came toward him. *"Who are you? WHO ARE YOU?"*

Just as my father was going to step into the pool, Mrs. Lardner came running up. Jeremy informed her that there was a man crashing his party.

"Nonsense," said Mrs. Lardner. "This is Ralph Chang, whom I invited extra specially so he could meet you." She straightened the collar of Jeremy's peach-colored polo shirt for him.

"Yes, well we've had a chance to chat," said Jeremy.

She whispered in his ear; he mumbled something; she whispered something more.

"I do apologize," he said finally.

My father didn't say anything.

"I do." Jeremy seemed genuinely contrite. "Doubtless you've seen drunks before, haven't you? You must have them in China."

"Okay," said my father.

As Mrs. Lardner glided off, Jeremy clapped his arm over my father's shoulders. "You know, I really am quite sorry, quite sorry."

My father nodded.

"What can I do? How can I make it up to you?"

"No, thank you."

"No, tell me, tell me," wheedled Jeremy. "Tickets to casino night?" My father shook his head. "You don't gamble. Dinner at Bartholomew's?" My father shook his head again. "You don't eat." Jeremy scratched his chin. "You know, my wife was like you. Old Annabelle could never let me make things up—never, never, never, never, never."

My father wriggled out from under his arm.

"How about sport clothes? You are rather overdressed, you know. Excuse me for saying so. But here." He took off his polo shirt and folded it up. "You can have this with my most profound apologies." He ruffled his chest hairs with his free hand.

"No, thank you," said my father.

"No, take it, take it. Accept my apologies." He thrust the shirt into my father's arms. "I'm so very sorry, so very sorry. Please, try it on."

Helplessly holding the shirt, my father searched the crowd for my mother.

"Here, I'll help you with your coat."

My father froze.

Jeremy reached over and took the jacket off. "Milton's, one hundred twenty-five dollars reduced to one hundred twelve-fifty," he read. "What a bargain, what a bargain!"

"Please give it back," pleaded my father. "Please."

"Now for your shirt," ordered Jeremy.

Heads began to turn.

"Take off your shirt."

"I do not taking orders like a servant," announced my father stiffly.

"Take off your shirt, or I'm going to throw this jacket right into the pool, just right into this little pool here." Jeremy held it over the water.

"Go ahead."

"One hundred twelve-fifty," taunted Jeremy. "One hundred twelve . . ."

My father flung the polo shirt into the water with such force that part of it bounced back up into the air like a fluorescent fountain. Then it settled into a soft heap on top of the water. My mother hurried up.

"You're a sport!" said Jeremy, suddenly breaking into a smile, and slapping my father on the back. "You're a sport! I like that. A man with spirit, that's what you are. A man with panache. Allow me to return to you your jacket." He handed it back to my father. "Good value you got on that, good value."

My father hurled the coat into the pool, too. "We're leaving," he said grimly. "Leaving!"

"Now, Ralphie," said Mrs. Lardner, bustling up; but my father was already stomping off.

"Get your sister," he told me. To my mother: "Get your shoes."

"That was *great,* Dad," said Mona as we walked to the car. "You were *stupendous.*"

"Way to show 'em," I said.

"What?" said my father offhandedly.

Although it was only just dusk, we were in a gulch, which made it hard to see anything except the gleam of his white shirt moving up the hill ahead of us.

"It was all my fault," began my mother.

"Forget it," said my father grandly. Then he said, "The only trouble is, I left those keys in my jacket pocket."

"Oh *no*," said Mona.

"Oh no is right," said my mother.

"So we'll walk home," I said.

"But how're we going to get into the *house*?" said Mona.

The noise of the party churned through the silence.

"Someone has to going back," said my father.

"Let's go to the pancake house first," suggested my mother. "We can wait there until the party is finished, and then call Mrs. Lardner."

Having all agreed that was a good plan, we started walking again.

"God, just think," said Mona. "We're going to have to *dive* for them."

My father stopped a moment. We waited.

"You girls are good swimmers," he said finally. "Not like me."

Then his shirt started moving again, and we trooped up the hill after it, into the dark.

HOUSE, HOUSE, HOME

THE CHILDREN OF COLOR LUNCH

No one was expecting that the children of color lunch would go wrong, and nothing on this spectacular fall day had exactly gone wrong yet. But Pammie Lee's small commitment to future world peace had landed her in charge of rounding up the children, and in so doing she had already managed two errors of judgment. The first was starting with the first grade. The second was leaving it to the children to categorize themselves by their internal reality. The result was that Kennedy Prescott immediately raised a fluttery hand and announced, straightening her London Zoo sweatshirt, that she would love to come.

—My au pair is from Montana, she explained.

Her sidekick, Ondi, best known for having dressed up as Madeline four Halloweens in a row, also volunteered, saying that while she had to check with her mommy, she was 90 percent sure she could make it.

—I'm pink, she concluded.

They then asked if they could bring something. Pammie, vaguely afraid they were thinking wine, put them in charge of juice.

Meanwhile, three black children whispered to each other in the science corner, in a way that suggested they might have an inkling that they were children of color. This impression was reinforced, somehow, by the fact that all three of them—two boys and a girl—were wearing black sneakers. Was that a racist thought? Pammie wondered, even as she sensed that the kids felt pre-empted. And why did they clump together like that if all was healthy in the school racewise? The four Asian American kids, too, seemed conspicuously inconspicuous. She suddenly wondered if any of the kids knew what a child of color was, and whether they were supposed to have figured this out for themselves. Surely someone had told them? Their parents? Their teachers? Maybe, unbeknownst to Pammie, it was her job; never mind that she had neglected to apprise any of her own three children of what they were. In truth, she was only on the diversity committee because she had thought she had had a miserable childhood like everyone else's, only to discover belatedly—now, in her mid-thirties—that her childhood had been miserable in a different way. That she had been, as a wag of a baby-sitter once put it, *margarinized.* This was the same sitter who had told Pammie that if she wanted to survive the 1990s, she should not use the word *oriental* except for rugs—something she would apparently know if she hadn't gone to a podunk East Coast college, stronger in foliage than in politics. It was something to think about.

So here she was, and who knew? Maybe the kids had been told and did know but had checked their internal reality and decided it didn't much matter to them. Maybe they liked their regular lunch, which they found comforting, or fun; or maybe they felt shy. It was hard not to notice that some of the Asian American kids were quite distinctly shy, whether or not it was politically correct to say so. Biracial Samantha Li, for example, was a star at Suzuki violin and read on the fourth-grade level, but she did not talk except during a book group she had formed, which met during recess. On the other hand, some of the Asian American kids were hell-raisers, for example, little Lester Young with the buzz cut. School rumor had it that he had slicked his hair up with Vaseline, only to discover that it didn't wash out; his parents had had to cut all his hair off. This only added to his mystique. He was not only, of course, a jazz great, as his parents found out when his name appeared on a postage stamp, but also a legendary soccer goalie— some kids said he used magic dust.

But when it came to a special lunch, maybe even he didn't want to be singled out in this way. Or maybe he, like the other Asian American kids, envisioned any lunch proposed by someone who looked like his mother as yet another tortuously overlong banquet, a continuous drone of a meal where you didn't even get cake at the end. Orange slices, you got paid in, or lichee nuts. All anybody ever said in English was either that you were very smart or else that you were getting so big.

Pammie sighed. The lunch, she decided, was too much about adult paradigms. All the same, she did the second grade, and the third, with what seemed to be better results.

Pammie's middle child, Phoebe, pirouetted into the lunch with her lunch box open. Her blue corduroy dress was sparkling down the middle—glitter glue, it looked like—and one of her braids had come undone. What with her straight slippery hair, this was always happening. Her whole face was smiling, though. She had her mother's triangular-shaped mouth and matching triangular eyebrows, but she had her father's big vertical smile, with a puckish tendency to roll her lower lip in over her teeth, so as to show off her saucy tongue. She had been this way since birth, it seemed—impendingly naughty. Even in the the hospital nursery, she had kicked her way out of her swaddling blankets, over and over, until the nurses finally gave up and just draped her receiving blanket over her bassinet. Houdini, Pammie's then husband, Sven, used to call her—more appropriately, it turned out, than he could possibly have known. Already disappearance seemed a theme of her life: Not only her father, but, for example, now, her sandwich was missing because, as she explained with great enthusiasm, she had donated it to the worm farm for an experiment. The worm farm was a cement cistern full of worms that the worm club had dug up in the playground. Since there had been some debate as to whether the worms ate peanut butter and jelly, or only dead leaves, she had put her sandwich over the top of the dirt with the idea that the worm club could check it the next day for holes or other signs of its having been eaten.

—It's an experiment! she said again, her eyes brilliant with excitement.

—An experiment! Pammie exclaimed back, despite an article that suggested that mothers with overly repetitive vocal habits were not doing the best by their children, language development-wise. But already Phoebe had gone on to explain how she was hoping it wouldn't rain and make the sandwich soggy—her nose wrinkled at that possibility—anyway, she didn't think it would. Though there were clouds in the sky, her friend Luke had pronounced them stratus clouds, a kind that didn't rain. Only cumulus clouds did. He said it said so in *The Magic School Bus.*

With this, she pranced off into the lunch, which was being held in the kindergarten, only to stop short at the sight of all the strange faces. She ran back to Pammie and took her hand, but immediately let go of it when she spotted her friend Luke, the weather expert. Then she was off once more, heedless of an apple that had rolled out of her half-zipped lunch box. Next came a piece of cheese in Saran Wrap. Pammie followed her daughter into the room, picking up her trail as fast as she laid it down, and in this way met Carver. A moment in most ways as unremarkable as it was undignified: Pammie was kneeling on the indoor-outdoor carpet, thinking partly about how she had heard it would eventually be replaced by tile—in time, she hoped, for her youngest, Inka—but also relaxing a bit, as she always did in this space. She loved the microcosmos of the room. So much busyness below—a warren of low bookcase partitions—with so much clarity above, and a suggestion of ocean in the extrabig sink—a curvy forties affair that looked to have been modeled after a bumper car. There were animals, there were plants, there were projects everywhere, and she swore that an inexplicably after-a-rain sort of light, very like a blessing, fell on this room alone.

Then Carver happened into view, a first man, perfect for child study. In truth, you rarely saw adult males in the younger classrooms, and that was part of the shock of him. Graceful; gentle; possibly a Pacific Islander. He had a face like a monk's, with a certain look of wise forbearance that involved the deliberate settling of the eyebrows; and he wore an earring—betokening, in his case, mostly youth, Pammie guessed. His monumentality was far more striking, especially when he knelt to better hear his small supplicants. One at each knee. A triangle. Pammie noticed that, of course. The way that, enormous as he was, he seemed to fall into compositions, this one as equilateral and harmonious as a Madonna with St. John the Baptist and Jesus. How is it that certain geometric arrangements produce in a person real emotion? Why are we moved by shapes and space, by qualities of light and color, by enlarging shadow? She had read tomes on the psychology of art, and yet the subject still compelled her, as did this man. This man fascinated her. But so many images crowded every moment, every day. His image was by all rights destined to fade, a loss to time like any other—the way he suggested peace just by the bulk of him, the way he filled the frame of her view, an end stop.

Later, though, she would recall him vividly, and all because when she shook his soft-skinned hand, he shook back with three fingers and a thumb. His forefinger stuck stiffly forward in a way which suggested injury, but which also made her think, in no particular order, *Gun, lesson, penis.*

—A fellow yellow person, he said. His gaze likewise seemed unusually pointed, and fixed.

—Yes, she said, as though it were still a major event to be met with a fellow Asian in this town. Impulsively, she handed him the apple that was in her hand, part of Phoebe's lunch trail. He accepted it with only small surprise. Then the fire alarm went off, and chaos ensued, and she found her attention floating.

SVEN, AS SHE RECALLED HIM

It was the odd incidental detail that got you. That's what her ex-husband would have said. He would have said, *We are never immune to such pleasures.*

Or else: *Could it have been the penile suggestion that piqued you?* Then he would have winked, and maybe suggested some piquing himself.

Her ex-husband was Sven, an iconoclast of indeterminate origins. In the ten years of their marriage, he almost never talked about his past; and, as his erstwhile student, she never gained enough parity with him to demand what he would have called the satisfaction of her curiosity. All he would say was that he had had in his time two parents, one of each sex, both commendable; and that both were now dead, like his one sibling, a brother, who had succumbed to meningitis at an unforgivably early age. And, of course, there were the two winsome wives thus far. (The big vertical grin with this.) He already had his signature star-white hair at fifty-two, when she met him. This he cut himself and never combed, so that it resembled Samuel Beckett's more than Andy Warhol's, and mostly served to emphasize his ever-boyish looks—his amusable blue eyes, and plummy veiny eyelids, and impressively regulation features. He always said that her face was full of subtlety, like a landscape of sand dunes. She had those cirumflex eyebrows, and a pouty mouth. But otherwise she was all gradation, up close; and from afar, she was a lovely, longhaired oval on an endless S curve of a body. His body, in contrast, hung down in a T from his shoulders, like a scarecrow's; and his face was diagrammatic, what with his plumb-line nose and his dead level mouth. His jaw, too, had a clean, easy-to-sketch quality. His bones in general seemed to proceed to their designated junctures without undue delay. He was taut and transparent and attenuated in a way that brought to mind the low light conditions of Northern Europe; indeed, he did not like sun and had no idea what to do on a beach. This posed a problem once the children were born, and would seem to suggest a certain joylessness. Yet nothing could be less true. Joy was his characteristic mode in life, so long as lotions and sand and things of that ilk were kept out of it. He lived to delight and be delighted—one of the first things that struck Pammie about him, coming as she did from a family that thought mostly about bills.

Sven did not see why they should not sleep in the living room. Sven did not see why people should not come in and out at all hours. Sven did not see why he should not wear other people's clothes, if they were left handy. And why not pick up someone else's camera at a party, and, holding it behind your back, snap the party scene you couldn't see? One day a friend honked at him as he was crossing a street, whereupon he lay down on the crosswalk and beseeched the friend to drive over him. Which the friend did; later, Sven said it was an experience he would recommend to anyone, that everyone should feel how deeply a car's undercarriage could affect you—as profoundly as great art, under the proper circumstances. Another day, he drank down with his beer a live bee. That was on a dare; nothing happened. He was not stung in the throat and asphyxiated. No one had to call the poison center or an authority on stingers; and this was, in a way, the point. Pammie learned from him how to have fun, that life was supposed to be fun, or at least that there was no point in not having fun. That as often as not, one's actions had no consequences. That was a shock to discover for Pammie. She had grown up considering the optimum use of every dollar and every hour. Every action brightened or dimmed the great drive-in screen of the future.

From Sven she learned that the future held no drive-ins anyway.

There was meaning in the worldview with which Pammie had grown up; later, Carver helped her see that. To be powerless was at least to know what you wanted. But there was freedom in Sven's view, a simple restless American freedom that could not help but celebrate itself. Or so it seemed to Pammie at the time. She thought him rather like Pippi Longstocking, only with a taste for the marvelous: This was a man fully capable of falling in love with certain types of papers and erasers. He made detours to experience certain curves in a road. If you asked him if he had enjoyed his afternoon walk, he might say, *Yes! There were such magnificent shadows!* and fall into reverie. Every August he made a midnight swim out to the middle of a pond to behold the shooting stars. *The Perseids,* he would muse. And always he would recount the myth of Perseus, son of Danaë, to whom Zeus appeared as a shower of gold. He would describe the unutterably beautiful though hugely damaged painting of Danaë in the Hermitage; then he would return to Perseus himself, and the killing of the Gorgon Medusa.

This swim Pammie did with him for the ten years they were married; and later, with Carver, she did it, too. Then, floating, feeling the arch of her back, the hang of her hair, she was the one to say, *It's the Perseid shower,* while Carver wondered what other civilizations called the same phenomenon. He seemed to see more than Sven did, or maybe just differently. When she and Carver counted shooting stars, he glimpsed the stars she pointed out (*Look—over there!*) as often as she saw his. With Sven, that wasn't true. She often caught out of the corner of her eye the stars he pointed out, but he rarely saw hers—which might have been a function of age and reaction time. Or maybe it was the nature of his focus: Sven's far vision was outstanding, especially at night, but his peripheral vision was weak.

The two men were so different in their tolerance of the cold water. Sven, whippet-thin as he was, could stay in forever. He claimed this was because his mother had hardened him as a baby by putting his stroller outside every day for an hour, even in the winter. Carver, being from Hawaii, had also been hardened in certain ways. For example, he was not afraid of sharks. In fact, he used to go surfing with sharks, he said. They were mostly friendly, except for the one who used to like to come up under people's boards and knock them over—a gray shark, this was. The islanders eventually killed him. But a shark was a shark; the cold was another matter. Carver always wanted to come in just as Pammie was beginning to make out some very distant stars, and to think about how far away they were, and whether they were stars at all anymore, or had long gone extinct, even as their proud rays paraded their brilliant heritage through the skies. Sven would have wanted to ponder that. He would have wanted to ponder what future generations were going to know about the universe that we could not begin to conceive, and whether they were going to be able to conceive his generation. Sometimes he thought about names and phrases whose meaning seemed to be leaking from them already. *The military-industrial complex,* he would muse. *Nixon. Antiestablishment.* How animating those words had once been! They were still animating. Yet how much less so. Had Pammie, for example, any idea what they meant, really? They were no longer the shibboleths of a vast belief system. And how much meaning life, correspondingly, seemed to have lost. Sven would have lamented that. He would not have lamented his lost academic career. Officially, he had no regrets about that. But he would have lamented his lost youth. It was miserable to be an ex-radical, he would say. It was like retiring to your life. One might as well have been an athlete. *Do you understand?* he would ask her, and she would say yes, but still he would sigh. *Someday you will understand.* Together they would have contemplated the black rim of treetops around them, so barely discernible in the low light that it seemed a thickened band of sky. Bats skimmed the pond. Every now and then Sven and Pammie would have sensed more than seen them, as if through a sympathetic echo-location. Sven and Pammie would have watched the stars fall and fall. *The eternal silence of these infinite spaces terrifies me,* he would say, staring into the sky—and adding, after a moment, *Pascal,* for her sake. Once, he took his bathing trunks off while he was in the water, wanting to be naked in nature. He let them drift down to the bottom of the pond, genuinely heedless of the pollution and minor expense. *I am alone,* he said. *We are alone. You are alone.* Pammie felt a fish brush her leg. She felt the simple chill of his words, deeper than the chill of the water.

And yet, maybe, finally, she was more like Carver, who would have deeply regretted parting with a pair of favorite shorts. Carver would have been looking forward to the enveloping soft of a beach blanket, and wondering whether they ought to have brought something warm to drink. And ought they make a fire and stay? He would not have wanted to talk if Pammie didn't. But if she did, he would have built a leaping live fire, seemingly out of nothing—this being just the kind of thing he was good at.

A SEDUCTION, LONG AGO

Pammie had once been the object of all Sven's rapturous attention. This was twelve or so years ago. He was teaching then; she was classically confused—ostensibly premed, taking art classes on the sly. She enjoyed the serenity, the composure of art. But more than that, she liked taking classes to no point. To have no particular aim was to open grand possibilities; even at her know-nothing age, she knew that. So she was surprised but not wholly unprepared when it began to seem to her that Sven—then Professor Anderson—looked her way at the finish of every thought. Reasonably, this did not seem possible, especially with the room darkened for the slide projector. What could he see? (Later, she would reflect on the acuity of his night vision as further evidence of a possible low-light ancestral origin.) She only knew that it did seem that he would make his point, look at her, then look down. She thought she must be projecting, or something like that; this was in her senior year, the year she took psychology to try and get straight some things her roommate, Muriel the tennis player, liked to claim. For example, that you look for your father in every man. *Think,* she enjoined Pammie. *Did you ever . . . ?* Pammie tried to recall instances of her father looking at her with dangerous intent in the dark. But all she could actually recall were images of her father arguing with garage mechanics who had tried to cheat him. Also, of her father ordering a certain neighbor to keep his dog off their lawn. At that point in the semester, she still sat in the right-back corner of the classroom, so that she could close the door if any latecomers left it open, and perhaps in this she was her father's daughter—a die-hard defender of the right and true against the insults of daily life, for example, dreaded hall noise. But when she began to wonder if Professor Anderson was looking at her, she switched corners. Left back corner, one seat in. That was because the actual corner seat was missing its armrest. She idly wondered how things like that got fixed, and whether the maintenance crew had a stock of replacement chair parts, even as she noted that her change of seat seemed to have no effect. She felt then in need of some small repair herself. The distinct embarrassed relief that overtook her was at least easy to cloak with avid note taking. There was a large canoe-shaped gap between the window shade and the edge of the window; outside, a spectral squirrel paused on its way up a tree trunk and seemed to gaze at her, too. Mocking her. She was paranoid, she concluded. Delusional. Meanwhile, Professor Anderson discussed the last of Titian's paintings, a pietà, which Titian had intended for his tomb, but which he did not live to finish. Was Titian really ninety-nine when he painted it, as he claimed, or only eighty-eight? Professor Anderson pointed out how Titian had included in the picture a small ex-voto—a portrait, such as might be placed on an altar, of himself and his son. He talked about their hopes for surviving the plague, the stench of whose victims permeated Venice at the time. He described how that stench mingled with the cooking smells, lingered until bedtime, greeted everyone all over again at dawn. How touching it was that, confronted with such an omnipresence, a man of Titian's age—whatever that was—should still be praying to be spared. How moving that, full in the face of his mortality, thinking about his tomb, he should still be painting, painting.

—Think of what Christ's as-yet unresurrected body must have meant to him as he rendered it, said Professor Anderson. Was there an afterlife? Was he right to have faith? Here it all is, his doubt and his belief, and, with it, the exquisite workmanship that might or might not have any meaning at all, but was by then a matter of habit. Is this not an artist? A man who paints because he paints? Who cannot tell you why he must experiment endlessly with color but only that he does?

Professor Anderson seemed to dwell longer than usual on his subject. He pointed out the disembodied hand extending up the column on the right—a transition to the next slide. Then he looked for Pammie, and, to her horror, lost his train of thought. The slide projector jammed; the nightmarish light of the suddenly empty screen exploded into the room. People began to talk. It could not be happening. Yet by the end of the semester, he was on the carpet vis-à-vis their involvement, even though it was she who presented herself to him one day as he left his office for spring break.

—I am on my way to my cabin in Maine, he said, with no preliminaries. Would you care to come?

He stepped off the brick path as he spoke, onto a small patch of gravel, to let some people pass. An archipelago of scrappy grass grew up through the stones.

Pammie stepped off the path, too, then, surprised though she was at how old he looked in the glare of daylight—much gaunter than in the lecture hall, behind a lectern. He had a gap between his two front teeth, and the skin pores below his cheekbones looked enlarged, like the indisputable ravages of an ancient wasting illness. Terminal nymphophilial acnioface, perhaps. Old Johnson syndrome. His eyelids were purply; he had bags under his eyes; the rims of his elegant nostrils glowed apricot pink.

Still she said yes, clearly and immediately, as she had known that she would—not unaware of how young and strong her voice would sound to him, nor how quietly approving he would be that she would go with him, as she did, without stopping home to pack. Where had she learned this narrative? And how could she have felt it to be new? One day that would be something to ponder. Also, whether things would have happened as they did if the weather had not been so tremendous. How many lives have been shaped, not by the accidents of the stars, but of the clouds? Of course, people made their lives, too. Their wills counted for something. And yet the vaulting beauty of the day had inspired her. It was several orders less astounding than being visited by a pure-browed angel replete with gold-leaf halo and muscleman wings. Yet to behold the heaven-high sky, the big noon light, the sudden, endless entrance of new green leaves—those leaves fluttering, first nowhere, then everywhere and everywhere—was to want to live a commensurate life. The leaves had a thin, vulnerable look; they fluttered so much more readily than the tough green leaves of summer; and this was not lost on Pammie. She concluded that there was something tentative in even inevitable change. How reasonable, then, to be brave.

She was brave. She was on her way to Maine without a suitcase—suspecting, quite rightly, that she would not need many clothes.

Their lovemaking began by the roadside somewhere, in his splenetic brown Volvo station wagon with its patched seats and floor vents—those were the holes in its undercarriage. He shared his soda with her in a tollbooth line, placing the bottle between her lips. When she tipped her head back, he ran his pinkie down her chin and throat, down between her breasts, stopping at her navel—the car before them had moved up, and he needed his hand for the stick shift. She helped him switch gears, her hand below his on the shaft; he smiled; they linked fingers, then let go as he took a swig of the soda himself. A bit of soda foamed up onto his lip. He slurped it in.

—I need a quarter, he announced. No, more.

And at the toll basket itself, he parked the soda bottle, with no warning, between her legs. There was the ding; the gate was rising; it seemed to her she could feel the bumps of the textured glass through her thin skirt. That was not possible. Yet she thought that she could, just as she thought she could sense Sven's breathing speeding up. It had begun to drizzle. He switched on the wipers, which seemed to be shuttling their attention back and forth. To him, to her, to him, to her. The highway was lined with evergreens now, a monotony of trees. There were in the world only themselves and themselves, breathing, breathing, in response to the wipers. To him, to her, to him, to her. She replaced the bottle with his hand, his elongated hand, which sought her with a gentle persistence that she recognized from his talks. It was the familiar thing in all that was new. There was so much that was new.

To begin with, the warm feel of his gangly body. He had broad, knobby shoulders, an ill-defined center of gravity, a tendency to clamminess, and a lovely, spicy smell. The sensation of youth and age was the biggest shock, for someone young as she was. Not that he was so old, in absolute terms, at fifty-two; but that was twice as old as she was—more—and he was early to gray. How could she not have been fascinated with the mostly gray pubic hair and the inexorably sedate pace of even this, their passionate first meeting? She had not slept with many men, but she knew enough to be struck by an unflagging quality in Sven's advance. He was agreeably flirtatious. Yet, freewheeling as he could be in the world, he brought to his lovemaking more method than abandon. That was his conservative streak; later, Pammie would see it in other matters, as well. His pace was deliberate. He savored each orifice, neglecting none. Pammie noticed that his penis had a crook in it, but this was probably not age. Certainly he was still a man of consequence, as they joked. It seemed almost odd that, fifteen mouths north of that still-impressive virility, he had, poor man, below his crunchy overlay of chest hair, a suggestion of breasts. So the professor was human. The breasts gave her a little power to balance his. They made her consider, too, for the first time, the tyranny of manhood. Not that she said so.

Later, she was to discover that he did not mind his breasts.

They were bigger than hers, he would claim, though not so tantalizingly reminiscent of a ripe Seckel pear. But that was later. What was apparent from the first was that he brought a connoisseurship to her body that no younger man ever had.

—What do boys see? he said. Opportunity. Satisfaction. They don't know, they don't know, they don't know.

Afterward, he took the weight of her head in his hands, cradling it, feeling her trust. He pulled on her neck, uncrunching the vertebrae—making her, he said, a Modigliani. Other days, he would set his fingers between the hollows of her ribs, or lace them between her toes. And always he would talk—demanding the history of every birthmark and scar, insisting she reciprocate, until they had mastered at least this part of getting acquainted—until they knew each other's major injuries, and where range of motion had been lost. There was an enormous beech tree outside his Maine cabin, with several cabled branches; such was the intensity of her focus that weekend that Pammie found she had committed the lower reaches of that tree to memory, including its major and secondary branching.

—Look, she said one morning. They had just made oatmeal with currants and maple syrup, and were eating it out of enamelware bowls, in bed. Sven's cabin was a one-room log structure dominated by an enormous window. The bottom edge of this fell so low as to give Pammie the feeling she could roll right out of bed onto the ground mix of green shoots and leaf mold. But the view up was of the tree; and that was what Pammie sketched now, from heart, with uncanny accuracy.

—You have a photographic memory, said Sven admiringly.

—I don't. But look.

—How extraordinary.

By the end of the weekend, *Would you care to come?*—the question he had posed as he stepped off the walkway—was a joke between them, with a host of variations. By the end of the month, he was reviewing everything that was distasteful about academia in general and his department in particular, that he might pronounce himself more freed than fired. How he would have minded the ignominy of his dismissal if he were not day by day finding her company—her being—ever more enthralling.

—The quality of your attention, he explained one day as they repotted plants. She had just moved in with him; they were enjoying their new domestic moments together, many of which were the belated rituals of spring—the removing of certain remaining storm windows, for example. The raking up of the previous year's leaves.

—That is with which you smote me, he continued. Smite me still. So simple and unwavering, as if everything in the world matters to you. As if you stand at the beginning of time.

She was not sure what to say to this, but accepted it as a compliment.

—A feeling creature, you are, he said, with no frozen-up parts.

—Thank you, she said.

Later, Pammie found out he was in a life crisis at the time— a midlife crisis that involved wanting to get away, while he still could, from controlling women.

She had no conception then that she would ever have frozen-up parts.

They made little people out of the extra clay pots that May afternoon, the sun so strong that their warm backs seemed hardly related to their cool chests. They stacked up small pots for legs, placed larger pots rim to rim for the bodies and heads.

—How very many people belong to the vegetable kingdom, he observed, and they categorized his various colleagues by their growing habits. One was truly weedy; another, a late bloomer; another, frankly, dead wood.

—A collection of cellulose, the lot of them! Herbaceous perennials! So he termed the specimens with tenure. Those without, of course, were mere annuals.

There was strain in his metaphors. Pammie worried as she laughed. One night, they had walked by a house with the shade left an inch high, and he had commented on how you could tell through even so narrow a slit how many people there were in the room, and whether they were moving around. Now he pulled his own shades down with precision, to a millimeter short of the windowsill. Should the shade actually lie on the windowsill, he pointed out, there would be gapping at its sides. It was important, too, to pull the shades before switching any lights on. He chastized Pammie for neglecting to do this the one gray afternoon she switched on a lamp in order to read.

—But it's nowhere near dusk, she argued.

It was, in fact, three in the afternoon.

His efforts to protect himself by and large succeeded, in that his colleagues shunned but did not wound him. It was, instead, the mailman who managed to make him feel like a pervert and a pariah. And the garbagemen—the articles in the paper said such monstrous things that even the garbagemen did not stand his empty barrels back on the curb anymore, but left them rolling around the sidewalk and street. A nightmare and a cliché—that's what Sven thought he had made of his life.

—I have always been a gadfly, he commented. Now I am a cradle-robber to boot. A nympholept.

Pammie could see how he felt, but experienced all that was happening as a life adventure still.

—To be the center of a scandal! said Muriel. There was envy in her voice. Pammie was living, not college life, but real life. Braving her last few lectures, she felt heady, spoken for, elect—as if a talent scout had picked her out, as if she were headed now for a big city.

She and Sven were married immediately—an aesthetic decision. For was this not called for? That they should be carried away, that the drama should broaden and lead on? He wore to City Hall, with a wink, a long face. She wore a pink slip.

—Until death do us in, he teased when he kissed her.

It was not a thought she had ever thought to have. She opened her eyes to behold the reflection of the louvered fluorescent light fixtures in his.

In attendance were Muriel and her new boyfriend, John, who good-naturedly blessed them with a tennis racket.

—I now pronounce you man and wife, he said. May you live long and remember to keep the ball deep.

The rice had to wait until they were all outside on the stone steps.

—Hooray! Congratulations! cried Muriel and John then, hurling fistfuls of grain into the air. After the rice, there were rose petals, and after the rose petals, confetti.

—Enough! Enough! Sven laughed, a foaming champagne bottle in hand. Which way to our honeymoon?

For the honeymoon, Muriel had dumped forty pounds of birdseed in an old church fountain; the idea was to be surrounded by hordes of pigeons as they flipped through Italian art books, pretending they were in Venice. There were café tables, with tablecloths; water was evoked by sheets of blue and green cellophane. Muriel presented them with a collection of gondolier pencil sharpeners, which they disposed among the waves.

—And, of course, music! she announced, producing a tape recorder and tapes. She had also brought an enormous hamper of Italian food, most of it fish-related.

—What do you think? said John. Should she go into the party-planning business?

—It's your calling! cried Pammie and Sven. We'll back you!

Pammie presented Sven with a set of leather masks she had found in a flea market. A sun, a moon, a Neptune, a Bacchus. They tried to wear these while eating the seafood lasagna, a challenge. In turn, Sven gave Pammie an antique Japanese raincoat, made of straw. It came in two parts, front and back, like a sandwich board, and caused much flapping and stirring among the birds when he lifted it up.

—See how tightly woven it is, he said. Enough to repel water. I loved the unexpectedness of the idea. A straw raincoat.

—Shall I put it on? said Pammie.

—It's for contemplating, he explained. You hang it on the wall.

—Just the thing for a nice Japanese wife, said John.

That was awkward.

—Chinese American, said Pammie, lifting a glass of Chianti. The air smelled equally of the wine and the musty straw.

—To the unexpected! said Muriel.

A priest with a thunderous footstep appeared, delivering a perfunctory warning amid many warm blessings. A newspaper reporter took their picture and names but asked how old Sven and Pammie were.

—Congratulations, he said.

Sven gazed after the reporter when he left.

—I'll buy a house in the suburbs if he runs that photo, he said.

The pigeons at that point were still feasting. There were other birds, too.

—Sparrows, maybe? said John. Robins?

—Those are definitely not robins, said Muriel.

Everyone was tired.

—How lovely it would be to leave this all here, mused Sven. A little contribution to the services tomorrow.

But Pammie and Muriel and John agreed that they should make no such offering. To begin with, that reporter had taken their picture.

—And that priest was so nice, said Pammie. We could dance away into the sunset, but at his expense.

—You go. John and I will have this up in a snap, offered Muriel.

John, though, looked surprised.

—Did I agree to be volunteered? he asked.

In the end, they all cleaned up together, with the perversely cheering aid of a most vulgar sunset.

Pammie wrote her parents that night to inform them of what she had done. *I hope you won't be too upset,* she wrote. *More has happened than I can describe. I wouldn't blame you for wanting to disown me, but want you to know that I am happy.*

MARRIED LIFE

Sven thought the idea of disowning very strange, being himself indifferent about money and possessions—commodities, as he called them. Yet all this leisure, this freedom to be rather than to do, to study shadows instead of stock indices took filthy lucre, as Pammie knew. Indeed, she sometimes suspected that his vagueness about his past was related to a reluctance to divulge either how he had come to amass the half million dollars he had in the bank, or how a yet greater amount had dwindled to this. He kept his money in a savings account. He did not know what a certificate of deposit was, or a treasury bond, or a mutual fund. Stocks bored him. Yet what did it matter? They lived at the beginning in a kind of delirium of freedom from such concerns, and from the past and their families, as well. Sven looked on his many overcomplicated relationships as threads in a winding cloth, some longer, some shorter, but all of a proven tensile strength. He shook his head the day Pammie described to him the number of family occasions she was used to attending, the number of presents and cards she spent her time planning and buying and wrapping and sending. Even as she spoke, the phone rang—her sister Celia calling about their parents' anniversary, and whether it wasn't time to start encouraging them to move to a smaller house. With a bedroom on the ground floor, she said. Also, what to do about their youngest brother, Andrew, who was depressed and had opened a joint bank account with a bulimic tap dancer; whether Pammie had started thinking yet about Christmas; whether Andrew could move in with her if things got worse; where Pammie was staying for their newest niece's baptism; and whether Pammie thought a twenty-five-pound turkey was going to be big enough for Thanksgiving if there was a ham, too.

—There were eight kids in my family, Pammie told Sven. That is, there are. Eight kids. And now there are lots of grandchildren.

She had to stop to think how many, and how old they all were, and when their birthdays fell, and was describing to him what she was planning to get for each of those birthdays when he began to ask, Is that how you want to spend your life, trying to remember and please?

—It's very nice, and that's fine, he said. Except that there is no such thing as a nice artist.

Was that true? By this time, she thought it might matter to her. She was hardly ready to proclaim herself an Artist, capital A. But the more she settled down, the more she realized that her work had assumed a new place in her life.

—Art is about originality of perception, continued Sven. It does not agree with society. It disagrees, always, as individuals in their secret hearts do.

She had never seen him so adamant. His Adam's apple plummeted to the bottom of his neck with a rapidity that alarmed her.

—There is no such thing as a nice artist, he repeated. And there is no one nicer than the daughter of an immigrant.

He held a watercolor of hers as they spoke—a small anti-landscape, with a pair of sheep with crosses for faces. They looked like woolly-bodied fencers.

—Fenced fencers, Sven quipped, suddenly less insistent—lost, for a moment, in that strange grassy world. Adam and Ewe in a garden for eating, he said.

He was right to joke. The piece was whimsical. And yet, as he pointed out, the light, democratically divine, touched the backs of the animals with a kind of sanctity.

—Complexity is good, he said. Clever is fine so long as it cuts deep. He nodded, as if in good-natured agreement with himself, then continued, You may yet prove the real thing.

It was rare for Sven even to verge on a compliment. Sven, after all, thought in terms of the Artist more than ever, as if, having left the classroom for real life, he was bent on turning real life into a classroom. Yet there was something in his ideas that was strange to Pammie. She loved to draw. She was alive to beauty. She thought she could feel greatness, and was grateful to be in its presence. But she did not think of herself as anything but a fledgling talent, with years of groping ahead of her. She had begun to go to galleries, and to read, and to become aware of the difficulties of painting today, after the advent of photography; after people like Marcel Duchamp. A knack for representation such as she had, a certain spontaneity, an openness to innovation hardly seemed enough. She could see the argument that art was done with representation; that it should not pretend to be more than paint on a canvas; that it should perhaps evoke a higher plane, a spiritual plane. She was interested in current ideas about appropriation, and deconstruction. She appreciated the questioning of high and low, and of the market. What did make an object art?

Only Sven seemed to think of art as a rendering of light and space and powerful personal perception.

—You read too much theory, he said. Just find the line of painting you would rise from your deathbed to continue. If there are figures in it, leave them there. So the canvas is flat. So perspective is a lie. So what? All culture is artifice. It's fine to make a new art of pointing this out, but artifice is what makes us human. It's ridiculous to try to do away with it. Rebellion against a dead tradition is a great thing. You have only to go to Paris to understand how ossified European culture had become, and how necessary it was to have a Picasso. Now what do we have, though, but so many rebels without causes? They are not so much moved to overturn what they feel to be dead as they are bent on overturning *something*, because they would like to be artists, and that is what artists do. They are anti-perspective and anti-representation, but if you ask them why, it is because those things are passé—they learned so in art school. Let them be Quakers, that is my view. Let them apprehend the world for themselves, instead of relying on the clergy.

—Let them be sixties radicals, in other words. Let them be anti-establishment.

—Exactly.

—They should listen to you instead of to your colleagues.

—They should listen to themselves.

Pammie was not convinced.

—How conservative you sound, in a radical kind of way.

—Don't think in terms of the labels. Just think.

So he said. But when Pammie, a few weeks later, was still deciding what to think, he was impatient.

—What you are wanting is nerve, he observed finally. This is perhaps a result of your class.

Your inferior class, she knew he meant. That was a shock. Yet it was a relief, too, to hear their difference acknowledged, even in this painful way. For in the acknowledgment, there seemed a promise of acceptance.

—You hoped to find a new home in me, he said another day. It is not transcendence and glory you seek, but something much humbler.

Did that not have the sound of meaningful embrace? Their loft at that moment had seemed full of light and harmony. There was a Mingus tape playing. The air smelled of paint and of the almonds she had ground for nut soup.

—I'm going to paint you, she announced. I'm going to stretch a canvas the size of this wall, and fill it with you.

—If you like, he said, moving her toward the bed. But first the model must have his fee.

—I thought you were working, she protested.

—And is this not working? He put his tongue in her ear.

She laughed.

—You are the easiest wife I ever married, he said.

Other mornings, though, he was less easily satisfied. Other mornings, he seemed bent on kindling in her an ambition appropriate to her supposed talent. He held up for example his first wife, Natasha the distinguished photographer, who had harbored desires to burst onto the scene, to remake the field with the force of her vision or die. If Pammie had not Natasha's artistic fire, though, it seemed she should at least burn with conviction like Sven's second wife, Bianca the world journalist, who had had to reschedule their wedding twice because of coups.

—And what about you? Pammie wondered one day. I have to believe you have ambitions of your own, or did.

But he insisted he did not.

—I was never going to be more than a permanent lecturer, and I most certainly did not care.

Was that true? And why would he never have been promoted?

—I never finished my dissertation, that was one reason. Perhaps, too, there were some who found me willful in my views—in my refusal to retreat to a four-foot square of turf, much less to defend it, as they did, to the death. "Insufficiently open to his contemporaries," they said. "Jack-of-all-trades, master of none."

Moreover, I was resented for my fantastic popularity with the students. "More entertainer than scholar." "An easy grader."

—Were you an easy grader?

—I was not, he maintained.

She did not tell him that the students, too, had believed that he was.

—And why didn't you finish your dissertation?

—Too many hoops to jump through. I was an untrainable dog.

Sometimes Pammie thought that Sven had married her as a way of leaving his job in spectacular fashion. Other times she thought he needed her to be an artist in order to justify his impulsiveness in marrying her. Often she thought both. Why indeed had he taken a wife who would never measure up to either of his exes? He claimed to have left both of them, and to be happiest, by far, with her.

—We will be buried together, he liked to say with a wink. I predict it with one hundred percent certainty. That is, if we do not bury each other first.

Pammie did not envision herself buried or burying; but eventually she found herself sharing his sense that she had something special to do with her life—something that went far beyond the expectations of her childhood. A year after their marriage, Pammie could not imagine even proposing to Sven that they seek common ground with her family. And was not that exactly why she, for her part, had married him, to facilitate her leave-taking? That's what Muriel had once said, and what she would probably maintain still, if they were in touch—if Muriel and Sven had not had a falling-out over the elitism of tennis.

But they had. One day Pammie had entered the kitchen to find Sven and Muriel gesturing wildly in front of the refrigerator.

—Look at the acreage required, argued Sven. Look at the little white outfits. What does it smack of but a landed gentry who can afford to change their clothes all day? And who can make a varsity team today who did not spend thousands of dollars on lessons?

—Excuse me, said Pammie. I'm trying to get some juice.

No one moved.

—That's not even the question, argued Muriel. So what if it is elitist. The question is, What do you care? Why do you need to point this out? Aren't you an elitist, too—you who have never had to work a day in your life for money?

—I've worked for money.

—But not because you had to.

—Stop it, you two, said Pammie.

—And you have? said Sven.

—Of course I have, said Muriel.

—Ah. Well, then forgive me, and do sign me up for tennis lessons while you're at it.

—I'm trying to get some juice, said Pammie again. Would one of you please move?

Muriel stepped aside at that point. Pammie poured her juice. Sven took the glass from her and emptied it in the sink.

—What is the matter with you? said Pammie.

—Menopause, said Muriel. And to think of the poor exploited oranges that were picked in vain.

—It's time for you to leave, said Sven.

—Don't go, said Pammie.

But Muriel was putting on her coat, and Sven was standing by the door.

—Glory to you on most high, said Muriel, as she passed him. And disdain for people on earth.

—You may choose between us, said Sven, closing the door, then turning to Pammie. His voice had no rancor in it; he could have been telling her they were out of milk.

Later, Pammie conceded that Muriel had never been anything like her. Muriel loved committees, for one thing. Also she loved Christmas. She collected Christmas sweaters, and typically spent months each year planning the decorations for the college Christmas ball. The suite was always littered with bells and bows, and boughs complete with pine tar. One year, she made an entire herd of life-size papier-mâché reindeer. Pammie liked the reindeer, and helped Muriel paint them with textured ceiling paint. They did nail polish on the hoofs, a classic Muriel touch, then suspended the animals from the hall ceiling with fishnet. Muriel, more than anyone Pammie had ever known, had a way with fishnet.

But she and Muriel had never been soul mates, it was true. Sven was perfectly correct in saying Pammie and Muriel would have grown apart sooner or later. And perhaps sooner was indeed better than later. Pammie could see Sven's point. Still, she could not believe Muriel had really abandoned her because of Sven. She called; Muriel insisted that she was the one who had been abandoned. They talked a few times more. The air did not clear. Now Pammie missed Muriel. She missed Muriel's enthusiasm, not to say her psychological insights. *PIs* Muriel used to call them, as in *Now I hope you don't mind if I share a little PI with you.*

For example, that had Pammie married differently, she would have had to separate inch by inch from her family, her parents protesting all the way. Why didn't she come visit? Why hadn't she performed this duty, or that? Instead, they let go of her at the first glimpse of Sven, as if put in a trance. Pammie might as well have joined an emperor's harem. *That art professor,* they called him, even though he didn't teach anymore. They quizzed her about art professors in general as if they were anthropological oddities. *Do art professors eat lunch? Do art professors eat breakfast? Do art professors eat supper?* they asked. *What kind of food do art professors eat when they eat? Do art professors sleep in regular beds? Do art professors drive cars? Do art professors fill up the gas themselves, or do they pay extra for full service because they are too lazy to get out of the car?*

Sometimes they quizzed Sven himself. That was until Sven ceased visiting, saying that he was not a specimen. What's more, he did not like being compelled to eat at dinnertime.

—It's completely controlling, he said. A friendly hostility.

—My parents come from a culture acquainted with famine. It's a form of selflessness to share their most precious resource.

—But one has no choice as to whether one accepts their hospitality. They don't listen to no. They ride gangbusters over one's boundaries. It's naked coercion.

Pammie likewise visited less and less frequently. Neither did she invite her parents over, understanding as she did that they did not want to come—that they would prefer not to have to register their shock. They had not disowned her. But even on home ground, at their own neatened house, with its complete set of designated wastebaskets, one for every room, it was hard for them to accept that their crazy daughter had gone crazier.

Do art professors do anything around the house, or are they like Chinese men, their wives do everything for them?

Do art professors believe in working, or do they believe in collecting unemployment like those good-for-nothing bums you see sleeping right on the park bench as if that is their private property?

She felt older than the rest of her family, a threat. When her sister Carol got married, Pammie was not asked to be in the wedding.

—I knew you wouldn't do organza, explained Carol.

—I would have for you, Pammie protested. You're my sister.

But it was too late.

Pammie wore a vintage man's dinner jacket to the ceremony, as did Sven. She also wore a web of seashells in her hair—an idea she had cribbed from Muriel. He accessorized with a boutonniere made of orange plastic frogs.

—What's with the getup? asked her brother Maynard.

—We hear you've gotten yourself a motorcycle, observed her brother Andrew.

Actually, it was a scooter, but there was no point in trying to explain. Pammie tried to talk to Andrew about the bulimic tap dancer.

—Is she moving in with you? she asked.

—Whatever happens, I can't make as much of a mess of my life as you have, he said.

She tried to enjoy the open-air party room, with its humble view of a half-installed golf course. The sod was cut in squares like carpet samples; the fertilizer, in a heap, strongly suggested itself, in certain breezes, to be of organic origin. All the same, Pammie was trying to address her lobster bisque when her mother appeared with an old schoolmate.

—This is my daughter, I don't know why she dress like that, said Pammie's mother, who was herself wearing a silver Chinese *qipao* and a large orchid corsage. And this is my son-in-law, who doesn't eat Chinese food.

—That's one way to stay nice and slim, said her mother's friend, clutching her beaded purse with both hands. Of course, too skinny no good, either.

—Actually, I love Chinese food, said Sven.

—Really, said her mother's friend.

—He's making a joke, explained Pammie's mother. He's an art professor.

—Very nice, said her mother's friend.

—Right now he has no job, but you watch. He'll get one, you just wait and see. Then they can have a baby.

—What? said Pammie.

—Don't worry, you will get pregnant, said her mother's friend.

Sometimes wait a few years is the best thing for everybody. Of course, wait too long no good, either.

Sven wanted to leave immediately, but Pammie insisted they at least stay through the cutting of the cake.

—What's the point? he wanted to know.

—It's my sister's wedding.

—And so?

Later, he acknowledged that it was at least useful to have those seven siblings, most of whom had gone on in more regular fields, and who led more regular lives. They came to visit Pammie's parents bearing Drāno and sealants, long-handled tools, tax forms. That was lucky. They made doctors' appointments. They explained what a computer and a fax machine were. They bought software. It was thanks to her siblings that Pammie could disappear once again and know that her parents were being taken care of. And was she not lucky, too, that her siblings for the most part kept their criticism implicit? As time went on, her two out-of-state sisters continued to call, but the other kids, more local, diplomatically kept their distance, pleading midlife busyness. Only her brother Wally openly shrugged.

—You dropped out, he said simply, in his disarmingly Wally-like way. He looked Pammie steadily in the eye, without blinking. Wish we all could live for art. It sounds great.

PAMMIE DISCOVERS HERSELF AN INTERESTING WIFE

If Sven did have an ambition, it lay for a while with a certain bohemian circle, with whom he fell in one afternoon at a café. Slowly, though, he and Pammie became bored with the improbable picnics and demonstrations of spontaneity. They became bored with the competitiveness of their new friends. All that endless wit. And cruelty—they became bored with the exhausting processes of dropping someone, or trying to keep in touch with someone who had been dropped, or had dropped out. Also, with the sneaky takeovers.

—We might as well have joined a department, observed Sven. Then we would at least be paid for what we endure.

One day they themselves dropped out, or were dropped, and then they found themselves with a drafty loft in which they had once hung a series of hammocks, six of them altogether, for friends to swing and sometimes to sleep over in. They took all but two of these down and, the space made, began to apply themselves to their work.

Sven commenced a study of Chinese art. This was not his field. However, he had grown interested in the subject since their marriage, and firmly believed that wonderful monographs could be written by nonexperts.

—It's a matter of sensibility and immersion, he said, excited at having found a direction, though regretful he had not discovered it earlier. So I am a man of ambition, after all.

He was interested in the experience of painting an enormous work once through, as the great scrolls had been painted—in ink on silk during the Sung dynasty, on paper in the Yuan. He was interested in the mind frame of an artist who could revise nothing.

—It makes every painting a performance, does it not? he said. Are not these literati painters more like dancers than painters as we understand them? And is there not a choreography?

He linked the choreographed nature of the painting to calligraphy. He theorized that a less demanding tradition would have proven less maddeningly conservative, though also less noble.

—The Chinese artist accepts the artifice, even celebrates it, like the painters of the Renaissance. You watch, he predicted. Something worth writing will emerge from these preoccupations.

Pammie suspected he was going to need more ideas and more

background to produce a viable book. Still, she listened and encouraged his reading and travel plans, even as she mulled over the turn toward Chinese art. So perhaps she was a wife who had brought something to Sven, after all. A wife like his others—an interesting wife. A suitable partner. Perhaps just as she had originally looked on his body with fascination, so, too, he had looked on hers with more than an appreciation of her firmness. He had always liked to comment on her color. In the winter, she was the color of the pith of a tree, in the summer, the color of a log floating in water. But wasn't that just Sven, endlessly marveling?

Perhaps she ought to have felt outraged by the sudden interest in Chinese art; later, Carver thought that. Later, Carver would hail this as proof that Sven had seen her as other, as not-self, as object to his subject, someone he expected to scrutinize, not to be scrutinized by. Carver would say these things and wait; Pammie had never known a man with so patient a manner. It was true that Sven had proven disappointed, over the years, that she did not know more about Chinese herbs, say. Also he had encouraged her to buy and wear Chinese dresses. But actually, Pammie felt more relieved than outraged by these things. She was glad to see Sven coming into his own ambition, for she was never going to be Natasha. In fact, she was in the process of abandoning painting altogether, and switching to architecture—an art about which Sven happened to know nothing.

—Is it possible that you are rebelling against me? he said.

—I would not rise up off my deathbed to continue what I'm doing, she said.

—You are in a lull.

—I have become interested in space, and in what it makes possible.

—Marriage has done this to you, said Sven. Sharing a space. Feeling a need for your own space. Or perhaps feeling how much more living space you have now than you did in your crowded home. Imagining who you would be if you had still more.

—Being married has sensitized me to these things, it's true.

—Moreover, you are at heart a practical person. You like the idea of producing something people use. The fine-art project is too airy-fairy for you.

—That is true, too.

—But mostly it is about rebellion. By going into space making, you make a space of your own. How elegant.

—I just find it interesting, said Pammie. I like the idea of working with people. And I like the idea of starting with a program, rather than starting with nothing. I find that a great anxiety removed.

—It's not about self-expression.

—Not so relentlessly.

—How very Chinese, he said.

She went back to school, where for three heady years she considered folded planes, free plans, nonaxial design. Tectonics, structural rationalism; thin-skin membranes, curtain walls, cladding in general. She learned to draw in a new way—to do figure-ground drawings. To use a mayline. Her drawings were beautiful and smudge-free, which her professors took to mean she had the discipline and will to realize her ideas. She read Ruskin and agreed that the ideal building should accumulate like a cathedral rather than be designed and executed like a death sentence. She fell in love with the Renaissance architect Alberti. Her buildings, she decided, were going to be like his, responsive to their human environment. Also, to their site. They were not going to be precious objects, verging on fetishes. They were going to see the world as much as they were seen.

Overall, she did well enough to dare, when she graduated, to hang out a shingle with her new buddy, Andrea. What an unheard-of thing that was then! For two women. As they enjoyed the ferocious support of their department chairman, though, there was work. Indeed, many people hired them exactly because theirs was a women's firm. Some clients liked making a political gesture with their commission. Some hoped for a smoother working relationship, with better communication, or for a deeper connection with the project. Others simply liked telling their friends they had hired two women. Two women! A novelty.

—I believe buildings start here, said one client, holding her belly. Men, you know, are empty in the gut. Women have many more parts. We are so very much more complicated.

That was Mrs. Edna Terhorst, who wanted her bedroom relocated underground. Andrea gulped down some ice tea to keep from laughing; Pammie chewed so hard on a pencil that the eraser came off in her mouth.

—Women understand about space radiation, said Mrs. Terhorst. Women understand bombardment. Men look at you as though you are crazy.

Pammie could keep her face straight during almost anything. That was something she learned about herself, a newly necessary skill, like knowing how to dress for different clients. Andrea taught her that. She would call Pammie before interviews and say, Tweed, or SoHo, or Gal next door, depending on what Andrea thought the prospective client would respond to. Butch—that was an option, too, which some clients seemed to expect.

—So let them think we're lesbian, said Andrea, managing to draw furiously as she shrugged. She wore her hair like Pebbles Flintstone when she worked, in a palm tree so tall that it hit her lamp and sometimes singed. For the rest of her life, Pammie would associate her partner with the smell of burned hair.

Being from a family of dog breeders, Andrea understood the world to be made up of the smart and the outsmarted, which gave her a certain ease in the role of handler. She knew instinctively what the client needed to hear, and could articulate that gracefully. Pammie, too, had inklings about what she ought to say, but felt compunctions about simply blurting it out. Andrea was clear about the role of architects in the world: to design buildings. If there was a moral aspect to their job, it was to supply good architecture to clients who would have settled for bad. She did not mind having clients who couldn't tell the difference, and she did not care if they were filthy rich. She did not mind talking their talk. Pammie did. Yet she was the one who intuited the needs beneath the talk, and made sure they were met.

Their differences made for a healthy collaboration. The commissions were small, and mostly domestic, with many kitchen additions and renovations. A children's playhouse—that was fun. A therapist's office. A no-frills beauty parlor. A bowling alley, and a kennel for a couple with a Saint Bernard and seven Chihuahuas. Andrea and Pammie made the final rounds for a host of competitions, and had hopes of eventually winning one.

Then Andrea became pregnant with twins.

—Twins! said Pammie. How exciting! Congratulations!

—I'm so sorry to do this to you, said Andrea, retching.

Andrea grew and grew and grew, until finally, toward the end, Sven took over as Pammie's assistant. He was taking a course in Chinese, but didn't mind holding one end of the measuring tape every now and then.

—What do you think? Could I have been a great architect? he asked.

He saw his stint as a great lark. As Andrea's leave stretched from three months to six to nine, though, the practice shrank. There were still some renovations. A few family rooms. Every now and then, Pammie was able to explore an interesting material—polished concrete, for example, in which she embedded objects. That was thanks to a neighbor with a connection in industrial fabrication. But no one could live on work that sporadic.

—Surely Andrea is coming back soon, said Sven.

—I don't think so, said Pammie. She appears under a species of house arrest.

—What do you mean?

—I mean that she barely gets to finish a sentence, said Pammie. She has to schedule time to take a shower. She eats baby food because she doesn't have the energy to get something out of the refrigerator.

—Is she happy? Sven admired a spiderweb in the corner of a window. Their loft, he had always claimed, boasted an unusual number of gossamers. It was like a forest that way.

—She says yes.

Sven squinted, shifted angles.

—But she falls asleep standing up. If one baby cries, the other cries in sympathy; and if one thing goes wrong, she cries, too, and can't stop. And where she never used to fight with Randolph, now they do nothing but.

—Over?

—He's gone back to work, naturally. His life goes on exactly as before.

—How churlish of him, to stick her with all the happiness.

—I don't think she would mind having some company. Isn't that what marriage is for?

—The unfeeling brute, to think of how to pay for the Pampers.

Of course, Pammie had known children were work, coming as she did from a big family. Yet having never imagined herself as the mother, she still felt surprise at the discovery. It was like stumbling upon a bed of ice pockets in a spring stream.

—You can't imagine what Andrea's house looks like. There are piles everywhere—piles of clothes, piles of mail, piles of newspaper, piles of diapers, piles of toys.

—A motif.

—But the babies are cute.

Pammie thought how to describe them, in all their strange babyness. How they kicked, and flailed their arms, and wore what little hair they had right off the backs of their heads. They were surprisingly wriggly and un-doll-like when you held them, full of passionate urges. One of the babies had nuzzled her breast, wanting to suckle it. How disconcerting that was.

One day, Andrea, breast-feeding both children at once, suggested that Pammie look for a job.

—We got the practice going once, we can do it again, said Andrea bravely. She cradled her babies under her arms like footballs.

—Of course, said Pammie.

She sent out her resumé. Also, she painted a little, and dabbled in media that Sven abhorred—tar, found objects, eggshells. Fart art, Sven called this. She found, with an exhilaration that surprised her, that she did not care. One phase involved scorching, then burning things in the fireplace. Sven tried to react to this less dismissively.

For his part, he was thinking now about looking at Chinese art as a species of religious art. Not just the Buddhist art, but all of it.

—Art with a program, as you put it, he said. The program is humanistic, but it is a program nonetheless, with ideals set forth quite purposely.

Had she used the word *program*? She thought the term his. Anyway, she was intrigued, even as she worried that his idea was not as original as it seemed. Then again, it could be.

—What's striking is that it is neither the absence nor the presence of a program that makes it art, but the artistry, she said.

Sven agreed, even as he busied himself with articulating just what the program was. Whatever he could or could not believe in, he at least had faith that the exercise of his brain was a good thing.

—A woman has only to think of others to be a woman, he said. A man without work is not a man.

They were happy.

ENTER THE CHILDREN

It was hard not to be touched by Sven's enthusiasm when, after some effort, Pammie also became pregnant. The miracle of life! Sven had a book full of pictures of babies in utero that he liked to rhapsodize about. Fantastic, magically lit pictures in which mysterious, veiny, bitter orange blobs resolved frame by frame into curled-up tadpoles, then into curled-up tadpoles with spinal cords, and then into huge-headed beady-eyed aliens with webbed appendages. Finally they turned, miraculously, into humanettes.

—Look, a vestigial tail, Sven said.

Indeed, it was fascinating to see that in the course of its development, the fetus recounted the ape chapter of human evolution.

—I once knew someone who was born with a tail, said Pammie. His parents had it taken off, but he remained unusually hairy and gymnastic.

—If our child is born with a tail, I think we should let him keep it, said Sven. I don't think it is the place of the parents to interfere with another being's body parts.

—But the social stigma, argued Pammie. The child's self-esteem.

They went on to disagree about whether they would let the child ride a motorcycle.

—The child cannot know how dangerous it is, said Pammie.

—Presumably the child is no longer a child, said Sven. If the child is old enough to drive a motorbike.

—But think how many things sixteen-year-olds don't know. To begin with, that they are mortal.

Pammie did agree with Sven, anyway, that these were important discussions to have.

—To discover the ways in which we are strange to each other, said Sven.

—But also similar, no?

Pammie marveled, too. Sven claimed she didn't, but she did. And she rhapsodized as well as anyone could while burping and peeing and trying to force down more milk. She imagined her child rolling down a grassy hill. She imagined her child playing ring-around-the-rosy. Those were clichés, she knew, but still she imagined them. Her child did all the things she herself had never done, being the fifth daughter of struggling immigrants. She imagined herself speaking kindly, always kindly to her child. Asking about the child's day. Baking cookies. Serving on the PTA. She was going to read her child *Winnie-the-Pooh*. Her brother Wally used to say that the world could usefully be divided between people who had grown up with *Winnie-the-Pooh* and people who had not. Her child was going to be the former. Her child was going to dress in the same kind of clothes everyone else wore. Her child was never going to be abused in any way. *In other families*, Pammie was going to explain to her noncomprehending child. *Not everyone is as lucky as you.*

By the end of her pregnancy, Pammie's belly lurched and rippled like a water bed inhabited by a harbor seal. Her back hurt. She could hardly breathe. She was repeatedly bitten at the tip of her belly by mosquitoes. How much bathrooms seemed to have shrunk in recent months! She could barely fit in them anymore. Perfect strangers felt free to put their hands on her belly, or to volunteer how very beautiful pregnant women were. In truth, though, she did not resemble the Venus de Milo so much as a Claes Oldenburg hamburger. Moreover, she understood why she had never seen a pregnant woman honestly depicted on a canvas. She ventured a few maverick self-studies—unsparing, close-up depictions of her fat-dimpled flesh, complete with leg spiders and stretch marks. That strange linea nigra, like a guide-line for being slit up the front of her shiny abdomen. The blue veins that radiated from her nipples, so that her breasts evoked the bugged-out eyeballs of a mad scientist in a cartoon strip. From across the room, the images looked like landscapes—pleasant scenes that grew disconcerting at closer range. The canvases seemed to grow bigger than they were, as if to suggest the way in which matters of the flesh could suddenly loom. The results were surprisingly poignant, and though Sven called them *women's art,* they did occasion, thanks to a neighbor, a small show and a few sales.

The summer swelled like a slow-motion storm, breaking records. Pammie's due date came and went. She lounged in super-markets, discovering frozen-food products of which she had been unaware. She carried a reusable ice pack in her purse. Sven bought a used air conditioner for their loft, a limited success. It was too small for the space. It blew a fuse if the lights were on. Still Pammie slept on the floor in front of it, in a complex of support pillows, listening to a funny *ga-link* that it made.

Ga-link. Ga-link.

Ga-link. Ga-link.

Then one day, just when she was beginning to think she might split open with impatience, Adam was born more conventionally. Later, she realized that she should have been paying attention to the details of her labor, that she would be sharing her labor story for the rest of her life. This was her Invasion of Normandy, after all. It would not do to be vague about which beach she had landed on. Yet how many hours had she been in labor? Too many was all she really knew. Her labor was induced; the doctor broke her waters; Pammie was sure the baby must be about to be born, what with the grip of the contractions, which seemed like something out of a sci-fi movie about body invasion. But instead of a baby— doldrums. Nonprogression. The Pitocin dripped. Sven read hospital pamphlets to her. *Gestational Diabetes: Questions and Answers. Infertility: Myths and Realities. Hormone Replacement Therapy: Pluses and Minuses.*

—I am going to have my hormones replaced, he announced. Keep my testosterone levels up.

He made paper airplanes out of the pamphlets. One of these unfortunately landed in the next roomette, which was populated by a party of transvestites. They were, to Sven's disappointment, not friendly.

—Leave them alone. They're worried, whispered Pammie.

—On the fourth day of Christmas, my true love gave to me: four drag queens dragging, sang Sven.

—That's not funny. Shush, they'll hear you.

They watched the curtain for disapproving signs.

Still she was two centimeters dilated. Back labor, someone said. Pammie begged shamelessly for drugs. In birth class, during any discussion of painkillers, she had always been the first to raise her hand. *Excuse me, but does that drug cross the placenta?* Now, she was waving her hand again.

—Excuse me, but is that the highest dose you can give?

—My Asian patients usually don't complain, observed the doctor, fiddling with her syringe. It's my Hispanics who cry and moan and act as if they're dying.

—How tactful of you to share that, said Pammie.

It was her one lucid moment all day.

The doctor had a neat oval head like a pill. An elegant woman with glowing skin, she looked as though she had just emerged from an herb wrap at a day spa.

—The trouble with a group practice, grumbled Pammie, is that you don't know who you're going to get for the big moment.

Then suddenly, she was six, eight, who knew how dilated, and Dr. Day Spa was barking, *You can do it, you can do it,* in a surprisingly low-pitched, raspy voice, like the voice of an auctioneer at the end of a long afternoon. She was wearing a green shower cap and what, on her, appeared to be matching green scrubs. Pammie was breathing breathing, doing her breathing; there was a tile missing in the ceiling above her; then pushing, she was pushing, breathing, pushing; she could not go on but went on—where was that from? The baby crowned, then shot out. An intern Pammie had not even quite registered was in the room caught him like a touchdown pass.

—Found this headed for the biowaste, he said, handing the baby to Dr. Day Spa.

A bloody, squirmy, marmy, piggly being was Adam, a melon child at the end of a most elaborate vine. He waaahed immediately in an unfruitlike way, then peed on the doctor.

—That's my boy! cried Sven.

Mysterious slaps and suctionings. Already, already he was being set to nurse. For this scrawny, bruised and banged-up, wizened little being not only had something on his face, still, but something on his little cone mind: lunch. He butted her insistently with his cheek, making gulping motions with his mouth. This was *rooting*, the sweet nurse said. The sweet nurse had a face shaped like a shield, but there was no defense in it. Then he *latched on*—that's what the sweet nurse called it. Pammie felt a tug and a pain like a bite at her nipple as he began to nurse. *A nip and napper*, the battle-ax nurse would say later. *But an easy baby, still*—so the third nurse said, reassuringly. The third nurse was the one with a stoop and her granddaughter's picture in her pocket.

—See how he looks at you, she said.

And indeed Adam looked and looked—mostly, lovingly, at her hairline. For that was what he could see, it turned out, where black met white, an area of high contrast.

Pammie agreed to let the baby sleep in the nursery, or thought she did. She was so tired, she couldn't be sure, though she did cry out, *No sugar water!* For she had read somewhere about the danger of giving the baby sugar water. What the danger was exactly, she couldn't remember, but she was definitely against sugar water. She remembered that before she fell asleep; and she remembered how she and Sven held Adam a few moments by the hospital night-light. He opened his eyes and, hearing their voices, turned toward them, then moved his legs inside his swaddling, a miracle.

—His eyes are blue, her family exclaimed when they visited. Blue, completely blue.

—They will turn brown, her mother said. I have seen mixed babies before, and their eyes all turned brown.

—I saw one whose skin was completely white, said Pammie's sister Celia.

—And was there something wrong with that? said Sven. If this baby looks like me, he looks like me.

—Of course he looks like you, said Pammie's brother Wally. He looks exactly, perfectly like you.

—Clearly, no one is supposed to say anything, said Pammie's brother Maynard.

Her mother left a basket of red eggs and a Chinese name, written out carefully in big block characters.

—Yadan, sounds like Adam, she says. It means Asia red.

—Asia red? said Pammie.

—That's what happens when you decide the English name first, said her mother.

Pammie's brothers and sisters left stuffed animals and bibs.

—Wasn't it nice to see them, in a way? said Pammie later. And don't you think Adam will want to know them as he grows up? All those cousins.

—He does look like me, said Sven, holding Adam up to the mirror. But with your almond eyes. Look at all the hair he has already. He has more hair than any other baby in the nursery.

—A prodigy, she said.

—Forget about your family, he said. He's ours. You know, the other day I saw a mixed child on the bus. What a handsome devil he was. Really quite striking.

—He's hungry, she said.

PAMMIE BECOMES A LOVE SLAVE

Adam! She held her minute leaky mammal with the surprising vocal capacity by the hour. She celebrated his every solidly successful burp. She celebrated and mourned his growing up, which started immediately. His umbilical cord fell off. His hair thickened. He grew expert at finding her nipple. No sooner was he a newborn than he became an infant; already she was retiring clothes. Then, hooray, he was learning to sleep through the night.

Pammie learned new songs: *The wheels on the bus go round and round.* This was through her exercise class, which Pammie was planning to paint one day—a large panorama, she was going to do, with many different interactions. Possibly in pastel tones like a Degas dance studio, only this would be *Women with Car Seats.* Some of the women would be in a circle doing pelvic tilts, their car seats in front of them. Some would have stopped to nurse, or to clean up some spittle, or to rummage through a diaper bag, while up front the instructor smiled beatifically. In real life, the instructor, Heidi of the asymmetrical hair, encouraged people to share their labor experiences as they exercised; this was when Pammie first realized she should have been taking notes. How long a labor, how long on Pitocin, any other drugs, asked Heidi. And did it end in a C-section, and did she have an epidural, and was it a walking or a total?

—Any episiotomies, or uncontrolled tears? Heidi wondered, circling her arms.

One woman had a forceps delivery. One delivered her baby herself, in a bathtub. One tore so badly, she had to go back for reconstructive surgery. One had drummers for her home birth, and a midwife who was supposed to be fabulously nurturing but who broke the baby's collarbone.

—That must have been hard. Heidi nodded at the end of the account. Thank you, she said.

Pammie tried to convey to Sven what the world of mothering was like. She described the freight elevators in department stores.

—It's like being an initiate in a secret society, she said. Strollers are not allowed on escalators, so the mothers all head for the back of the store. Then there we are, ascending, surrounded by moving quilts.

—Moving quilts are so beautiful, commented Sven.

—They are, agreed Pammie. All those sea greens and ochers and midblues. I love the zigzag stitching.

At least Sven grasped that part of her experience. Other parts, though, he simply could not fathom.

—Once you were the easiest of my wives, he complained. What's happened to you?

She didn't know what to tell him. And when was she going to get her body back?

—I wish I knew, she said. Andrea says never.

—Of course I love you still, he said.

·   ·   ·

Adam began to take cereal. His poop changed from a sweet mustard paste to real turds; his eyes, as Pammie's mother had predicted, turned brown. He weaned himself at thirteen months. Then suddenly he wasn't a child whose age was told in months. The baby who had nipped and napped; slumbered lightly; hiccuped with his whole body, for an eternity at a time, began to seem not so much a collection of physical traits as a personality— an otherworldly and attentive child, much like Sven. How thoroughly he examined his toys! Sven, smitten, made lovely wooden boats and whales and rocket ships for him.

—You are a magical child, he told Adam. You are a child of vast powers and irresistible charm.

And in this, Sven appeared to be right. Even Pammie's family embraced Adam, after a fashion—attending his birthday parties, sending him presents. They exclaimed, in letters, over his pictures, as if he lived overseas.

THE FUN HOUSE

With Phoebe, two years later, everything changed again. Adam sulked; Sven withdrew. Where he had often brought Adam to Pammie for night feedings, snuggling rapturously with Pammie as she nursed, he left Pammie and Phoebe on their own. And no hand-carved toys for Phoebe; she got Adam's.

—Didn't you agree Adam should have a companion? Pammie asked Sven.

—I did, he admitted.

—So where are you now?

—I'm here, he said.

—I can't tell.

—Well, I am.

Where had Phoebe's high energy come from? It was hard to

know; from neither of them, it seemed. Far easier to see was where it propelled them—out of the loft and into a house with more room. A most delightful house, if you overlooked its total lack of insulation, which Pammie probably would not have, except that they could not get a mortgage to build themselves, and anyway, there was no land. Plus, it was impossible to imagine Sven living in anything else but this: a fifties utopian affair, with all manner of sliding doors and partitions, most of them translucent; and with many, many windows, all openable, of course. There was never such a house for handles and finger holes. Every surface invited owner participation.

—Look how it perches on the land, said Sven, the first time they visited. Like a dragonfly.

The realtor, a composer on the side, wore a vest printed with eighth notes. He encouraged them to close their eyes and listen. The house resounded with wind and birdsong.

—This is what people with children do, he reassured them. Obsess about real estate. Next comes school and hoarding toilet paper rolls for craft projects. Don't worry, it's normal.

They liked this realtor, with his unkempt hair and basset hound body.

—I have children myself, he said. Look at all the living space.

They looked—admiring how the flow of traffic could be adjusted, the flow of air, how light could be bounced this way and that. There were some walls, but many suspended panels, too, on tracks. Sven pulled these about, marveling.

—You can rearrange the rooms, said the broker. You can break up the space however you like.

—A configurable house! said Sven. How completely delightful.

The configurable was in a suburb such as Sven would never have agreed to live in, except that parts of the suburb were quite rural, and their part of the rural part of the suburb had been organized many years before into what was, at the time, thought of as a loose commune. A precursor to the condo association, Sven called it, and perhaps it was, except that it had a vaguely Quaker-like feel, with everyone tending toward the spiritual side, and toward an interest in yarn. Sven said he had never seen such a group for hand-spuns, perhaps they really ought to take the communal playing field and turn it back into a sheep pasture. But in fact he enjoyed having a dip in the pond. How healthy, too, for the children to be able to run and roam around! Besides, there were magnificent woods in which they could all go for walks—woods thick with mauve-trunked pines and beds of moss fur. There were precipices and hollows for hideouts. Its dramatic rocky outcroppings glittered with ice pockets in the winter. The town schools were good, too—something Pammie and Sven had to think about now, hard as it was to imagine the children at a desk, seeing as how they had only just graduated from pants with leg snaps.

But though it had not been ruinously expensive to purchase the configurable—it was too eccentric and impractical for most buyers—it was expensive to live in the configurable, more expensive than they had thought. Uncomfortable, too. Soon they found themselves struggling with what Pammie termed the solar gain and solar loss. But whereas the physical discomfort united them, the financial discomfort did not. As they budgeted to insulate the roof, and then to replace the windows, Sven could not help but wonder how Pammie could have failed to see this problem coming. Wasn't she an architect?

—This is why doctors do not treat their own parents, she answered. They lose their objectivity.

Sven said nothing.

—I couldn't imagine you in a cozy little cape, she said. People make real estate mistakes all the time.

It was at least with a feeling of mutuality that they started to call the house *the fun house.*

—It mocks us, Sven said, with its air of being at our service, when in fact we live in service to it.

Now that he was officially against the house, he found that he had come to hate its flexibility, too. First of all, because it was not flexible enough. On account of the track layout, the rooms tended to line up enfillade, with one room opening onto the next, and with no hall. Also, he found himself perennially unable to protect his study.

—It seems that critical panels are always being borrowed for other uses, he complained.

That was easily remedied, but not before it began to become apparent that even with adequate space, there were new shortages that precluded the development of his work—namely, quiet and time and, worst of all, a certain mental availability—the freedom to follow a hunch out.

—Immersion is impossible, he said. Intensity.

Pammie reminded Sven of Vermeer, who had painted those subtle pendant silences while living with no money in a household with eleven children.

—It is an underappreciated aspect of genius to be able to imagine a great silence where there is none, answered Sven. I suppose one may conclude, too, that I am no genius.

Pammie put her hand on Sven's. But what was there to say?

For want of other choices, Pammie went to work for an architect who believed chiefly in exposed brick. Also, in exposed pipes. Pammie would have been happy to call their difference a philosophical one if only Dean Roberts could have been said to have a philosophy. Not that she minded exposed whatever. But he seemed to think there was true defiant cutting-edge honesty in the eschewing of wallboard, whereas she did not kid herself. Once you saw it in home-style catalogs, it was fashion.

—How about if we expose the brick right here? he liked to say to clients, with an air of expecting them to nod in response. *Now that's architecture.*

Pammie could only hope that she would be forgiven an occasional subtly mocking remark, given that she was being paid like an artist, i.e., with no benefits. And hadn't she become friends with Dean's wife, Dixie, who thought the brick business funny, too?

—Of course, we'd all rather be working in a wonderful little art house, said Dixie, spiking her diet Pepsi with rum. But who can afford it? We have kids. We have a mortgage. And how talented were we, in the end?

—It's a question, sighed Pammie.

She was beginnning to wonder if her own true gift wasn't for household management. Mrs. Vermeer, she called herself, as she feverishly acquired bins and baskets and canvas bags; every one had a designated use. Now that she had two children, she began to understand why her parents, with eight, had so many rules. She devised routines for buying winter gear (in January for the following year); for clothes washing and folding (a load a day, with whites every other wash); for grocery shopping and cooking and freezing (she was on the lookout for a good used freezer). For keeping track of family photos, she had file boxes of two sizes, one for the negatives and the other for the photos in chronological order.

—On the sixth day, Pammie separated the Tinkertoys from the Legos, quipped Sven.

—And she saw that it was good, said Pammie, adding, It's nice to hear you joke about something.

—Don't I joke anymore? Sven raised an eyebrow. Of course, you are a river of bons mots yourself.

—Andrea warned us about this stage of life, Pammie said. Remember? A joyous deprivation, she called it. She said the key was to keep track of the joy, and make sure it outweighs the deprivation.

—As it does, of course, said Sven.

They focused with delight on Adam's room-long pictures of bug parades. At three and a half, he had a myriad of interests already—in bugs, in fire engines, in trains. He knew what a coal tender was, and a roundhouse. He knew that cinders could get in your eyes. Phoebe, meanwhile, toddled everywhere, chasing her brother. *Am!* she called him, and sometimes *Mam!* To which he would answer, *I'm not a ma'am, I'm a sir.* Phoebe refused to sit in a stroller anymore. She learned to shrug like Adam, to thumb her nose like Adam. Adam tried to teach Phoebe to use the potty, donating a pair of his own underwear as incentive. Phoebe offered Adam spoonfuls of her cereal.

—Goo' girl! she cried when he ate it.

—This is it, this is life! said Sven, watching Phoebe smearing finger paint onto Adam's back.

Sven claimed to feel the fascinations of parenthood. He pronounced himself infinitely touched by the beauty of the children, by their vulnerability and sweetness and innocence. He took magnificent pictures of them, capturing their dual membership in the recognizable world and in another, more miraculous sphere.

But being older, Sven was more sensitive to disturbance than Pammie. That was true, too, he said. Moreover, he was coming to realize that, workwise, he could not wait for the chance that would come when the children were grown. It came out one day that all his life he had felt owed more recognition than he had received. He had not appreciated being considered a brilliant crackpot.

—The proverbial jury deadlocked on me, he said.

—I thought you didn't care.

—I might have thought so indefinitely. You were the one who convinced me otherwise. Remember?

The monograph was turning into something substantial. The monograph was going to be his vindication, or, at the very least, the work that would confirm something of significance to himself.

—I do not want to lie on my deathbed full of regret, he announced on his sixtieth birthday.

He had blown out his candles, with Adam and Phoebe's help, but now sat staring at the cake without cutting it.

—The children would like some cake, said Pammie.

—Ice cream! cried Phoebe.

—Perhaps I should cut it for you? said Pammie.

He nodded miserably. Pammie cut.

—Are you sad, Daddy? said Adam. Are you sad?

—Ice cream! yelled Phoebe again.

—Adam made you a picture book, said Pammie.

At least the book made Sven smile.

—Only two pages in this book? he said.

—Length isn't everything, said Pammie.

And indeed, the pages were wonderful. For Pammie had asked Adam what he thought Daddy wanted, and he had answered two things. The first was, *More sleep!* To illustrate this, Adam had drawn a picture of a sleeper car on a train, with Daddy and himself in it. Also he had said, *To finish his book!* And to illustrate that, Adam had drawn himself and his daddy reading a big yellow book.

—And what's the book about? Sven asked Adam.

—Trains, said Adam.

—That should be your beautiful book we're reading, said Sven. It's wonderful. Thank you. I love it.

—Ice cream! yelled Phoebe.

—She keeps on yelling, complained Adam.

Sven seemed happy until the children went to sleep. Then he turned morose again.

—You are some distance from your deathbed, said Pammie.

For inspiration, she pointed out their neighbor, Katherine, who was still going strong at ninety-two.

—Katherine lives alone and goes for a walk every day, no matter what the weather, said Pammie. She says she eats spinach at every opportunity and that that is her great secret.

—Look at my teeth. I went to the dentist today. My teeth are rotting.

—I was not aware of bridgework as a leading cause of death.

—It's easy for you to joke. You'll have time yet when the children are grown, he said. I want to lie on my deathbed knowing I at least did what pittance it was given to me to do.

He did think of the family. As their finances worsened, he gamely agreed to look for a teaching job, humiliating as that was. He tried, too, to be more thoughtful with the kids. Pammie had been trying to explain a number of things to him for some time—that Phoebe's nap schedule had to be respected, inconvenient as it was. That he needed to set clear limits, which he must expect to have tested. That he should not give in to tantrums unless he wanted more of them.

—You want to give your instructions in as neutral a way as possible, she had explained. Yelling is just reinforcement. It's a form of reward.

Only now did he begin to take her direction to heart.

—I'm parenting by the book, he claimed. I'm present and prepared and patient. The three *p*'s.

But Pammie continued to feel that she was forever walking into a room filled with crying and projectiles.

—When the children are cranky and controlling, you become

cranky and controlling yourself, she said. You might as well be a third child.

Plus, yes, she could pursue her work later, but she thought it unfair of him to hold her youth against her. What about her? Hadn't she agreed to spend her most vigorous years with a man who might turn out to be like Titian, still working at eighty-eight, but who was more likely, as he himself feared, to turn old?

SVEN HEADS NORTH

The opposite of marvelous had always been bourgeois. That was the label they had used for Pammie's family, for example. Sven used to call them people whose ambitions could be satisfied in department stores. But now Pammie was bourgeois, too, and so were all of her ideas about child rearing, particularly the ones that involved making sure the children were part of their community. Why should Pammie sit through every one of Adam's soccer games, for example? What were sports, anyway, according to Sven, but an introduction to competition and gamesmanship, a suitable preparation for careers in capitalism?

—In Bali, people wander in and out of dance and puppet shows the way we wander in and out of football games, he said. Their live culture has everything to do with understanding and carrying on their traditions, rather than with legitimizing brutality. Is this what we believe in, the diffusion of responsibility that comes with team play, and that allows people to grind one another into the AstroTurf? Do we want to teach Adam to disassociate himself from the real goings-on, the broken bones and ruined backs, that he might cheer? That he can grow up to exploit others without feeling much about it? And so what if nonparticipation puts him on the outskirts of his peer group? Aren't you just going because the other parents go?

Pammie denied this at first, but they both knew that if the norm had been for the parents to stay home, she would have gladly stayed home. They knew, too, that in her heart of hearts, she would just as soon Adam ran around in the woods for fresh air and exercise. She would just as soon he discover beaver dams and anthills. As she explained to Sven, though, she didn't want Adam to feel he was different from the other children. It was bad enough that he was as mild-tempered as he was. She didn't want him to feel his family was weird.

—Fear of the weird, said Sven. If this were *Jeopardy*, that would be the answer to the question, What defines the bourgeoisie?

—He's a child, Pammie argued. Children need to feel they belong.

—Shouldn't we bring him up according to our own values?

—You cannot expect him to reject society before he has mastered it.

—Better he not internalize ideas it will take him years to ferret out. Better he stay free all along than to have to liberate himself later, as I did. It is no simple matter, you know. Takes decades.

—Better that he never suffer as I did as a child. I was an outsider from the start. I know what that means. You spend your life getting over it.

They argued then about who was more genuinely an outsider, he who had had the vision and will to refuse an acceptance that was his birthright, or she who had been born on the margin and only quite slowly earned a conditional pass.

—If you've never felt even a pang of yearning about acceptance, you are not really an outsider, she maintained. Your brand of alienation is romantic and sentimental, and I resent it.

—I am sentimentalizing nothing. Our society is about the issuing forth of products via division of labor and efficiency-generating competition. It is dehumanizing and I reject it utterly, that's all.

As she would like to, also; and of course she would like to see the children do the same.

For a moment, they were in balance.

—But how can you reject society utterly and still have a roof over your head? she said. Unless someone in your family has left you a plot of land, say, and unless you are able-bodied enough to farm it yourself. Ask any immigrant how easy it is to save up for that plot of land, though, and whether you can count on being able-bodied. Better that we bring the children up to grudgingly accept society, don't you think?

—Touché, he said. But is it not true that you, Pammie, care not only to survive in this society but to have a place in it?

She could not deny this.

Could an elective outsider ever know what it was like to be the other kind of outsider? And did Sven not have, besides his education and money, a certain amount of social capital he could dismiss exactly because it would always be his? His looks and height would always connote power in this society, Pammie argued. Moreover, he had the air of presumption, a quality everyone recognized. She pointed out the way he looked over the renovation of a neighbor of theirs, striding right into the rooms, picking up objects, using an openly evaluative gaze. Meanwhile she, the architect, stayed close by their guide and looked about appreciatively. He was a person who would never be kept waiting while someone behind him was served. He had never had to say, Excuse me, but I was here first.

—You're too timid, he said. You are young. I ought not to have married someone so young.

—Your confidence was conferred on you by society. Your children do not look like you and will be granted no such thing. We need to think what the sources of their power will be, that they will not be constantly kicked by little people trying to make themselves feel better.

—What little people? he said.

—Touché, she said.

—Bourgeois nonsense, he said.

For some weeks after that, they hurled things at each other. They did also, at Andrea's behest, try a range of herbal remedies— minisilos of supervitamins and Saint-John's-wort, dropper vials of flower essences and kava kava. All these things were accompanied by beautiful leaflets that in themselves induced feelings of peace and well-being. Their line drawings were rhythmic and sensitive, evocative of mountain meadows; they made Pammie want to take up bird-watching. Sven, less charitably, called them potholder art. Still, he took the whatever gamely, only to continue putting his fine-boned fist through various walls. He knocked over a bookcase full of books. He smashed vases and mugs.

More and more, they hated themselves and each other. They hated what they were discovering about themselves and, worse, what they were doing to the children. Adam all but gave up sleep. Phoebe's preschool teacher reported finding her rocking alone in the corner of the classroom at recess.

—This cannot go on, said Pammie finally.

There was no divorce settlement. In lieu of child care, which Sven did not think he could pay, he wrote a statement giving up his share of all jointly owned property, including the house. This he had notarized. Then he packed up the old Volvo with some clothes and his typewriter. He was planning, he said, to live in his cabin in Maine, unwinterized as it was. He was not planning to put in a phone, or plumbing, or electricity. There was something in himself he had lost touch with, something essential that he thought might be restored to him through the offices of nature.

—How are you going to do research up there? asked Pammie. How are you going to study Chinese? Don't you have to travel?

No answer.

—And what if you get sick? You cannot go on living a lie at your age, but I wonder if you have a choice.

—Of course I have a choice, he said. One always has a choice.

She realized later that she had assumed his age would stabilize their relationship, that his increasing vulnerability would make him more likely to accept imperfections in his living arrangements. But, of course, that was exactly wrong: People fight the specter of dependence, if only to feel the strength of their resistance.

She realized this much later. At the time, she was too busy to realize anything. She was too busy missing Sven, and the texture of their companionship, which had indeed had its marvelous days; and too busy with coping with a third pregnancy. This was for some reason much more of an insult to her body than the first two had been. Her morning sickness was not as bad, but her varicose veins were worse, and she had sciatica to boot. Sven had helpfully accused her of getting pregnant on purpose, but truly she had not. She had simply never quite registered before that a diaphragm was less than 100 percent effective. Also, she had refused to get an abortion—a fact that made the child, in Sven's view, her child. This was not why he left. He said so quite clearly.

—I am leaving because I cannot call this existence we share a life. These are my precious few years on earth. I do not cede them to you.

The Volvo, as it set off down the road, looked the same as it had the many times he had driven it around campus, or to town, or to school. Its back lights flashed several times, as if sending a message in Morse code, or as if he were about to stop. But that was just Sven's recently developed habit of riding the brake. There was no message; he did not stop.

.   .   .

Two months later, Pammie was fired from her job. Dean didn't have the courage to call; he made Dixie explain how Pammie seemed to be the ringleader of an office counterculture. Here Pammie thought of herself as washed-up, wrung-out, all but petrified by her abandonment and pregnancy. Still, according to Dean, via Dixie, it was as a result of Pammie that people took group bathroom breaks of a loud and extended nature. There had been several three-hour birthday parties with exposed-brick motifs; people had put pictures of Dean in their computers as screen savers; they took vacations on short notice, sending back ostentatiously bland postcards that appeared to be in code.

—I did try to get you severance, finished Dixie.

Pammie was forced to call her parents to ask for a loan, which they generously and immediately but silently supplied. And not too long after that, she went into labor, three weeks early. Andrea and the twins rushed over to baby-sit; Dixie, like the true and eternal friend she genuinely intended to be, sped Pammie to the hospital. Dixie brought with her a variety of scented lotions, as well as a spectrum of nail polish shades, in case there was a lull. But there was no lull. This time around, Pammie tried laboring in the shower. She tried for the first time, too, a squatting position. A birthing chair. These things were a distraction, if not a help exactly.

THE DOG HOUSE

Pammie developed a certain tone around this time. It was brisk and no-nonsense with a humorous edge—a surprise and a source of wonder to her. She had always been so visual. It was not something she would have expected, that she could find satisfaction in the mastery of a tone—out of, say, making a little less much of marvelous shadows encountered on walks. This manner was a kind of deception. She knew this herself. Yet it gave her a handle on her circumstances, which might have otherwise rendered her bitter, and if that was a rationalization, she was happy to have one. For at the moment she had more appreciation for a good realtor than for emotional range, and she would certainly have traded off more than a few more nuances of feeling for a cheap, reliable sitter.

Or how about a good wadder? She had never done so much wadding as she did now, packing up to move from the fun house. It was certainly a challenge to the creativity to do this with a two-month-old and two mutinous helpers. Sleep, she thought, sleep. All she could think, as she leaned into another box, her Snuglied baby propped against its edge, was about sleep.

The dog house was so called because several of its previous tenants were dogs whose considerable scented legacy had scared off many a moderately motivated buyer. This made for a quick and easy transaction such as it never would have occurred to Pammie to seek if it weren't for Dixie. But Dixie had heard of the owner's desperation, and had witnessed, of course, Pammie's; and she had reasonably concluded that this deal was the answer to Pammie's money woes. She laid it all out for Pammie in a way that Pammie thought made sense, as best she could tell through her exhaustion. By selling the fun house and moving to something smaller, Pammie could float the family through a year, even two, of no work. Staying in the same town meant that the kids could stay in their same schools, and keep their same friends. They could keep their same pediatrician and same dentist and same park, not to say their favorite sledding hill, with the turn Adam had finally learned to negotiate. What did it matter if the dog smell defied Lysol? Dixie and, therefore, Pammie had faith that the aroma would eventually dissipate, like the lingering whiff of that other dog, Sven.

How Sven would have hated the house! A one-hundred-year-old center-entrance colonial, it had last been updated in the twenties. All the utilities were on the ground floor. The bathroom included a bathtub but no shower, a washing machine but no dryer. The kitchen sink backed up to the bathroom. The living room measured ten by twelve. The molding was mostly one-by-fours, the floor a sort of figured wood—antiqued by the dogs, it seemed. However, the original woodstove had been replaced by gas heat, and the storm windows worked, and the house was well insulated—a shelter. In it, the family clustered together. The closeness of the arrangement would have driven Sven crazy. There was certainly no room for anyone to be pursuing higher endeavors involving, say, thinking, unless he wanted to do it in the garage—where there were, oddly enough, a sink and some shelves, suggesting a former darkroom. For Pammie and the children, though, the house afforded a sense of being almost literally in touch.

—It's like a submarine, said Adam. Except that instead of bunk beds, we have regular beds. And we don't have to sleep in shifts.

The submarine feeling was unhelpful if baby Inka was up with an ear infection at night, or if Phoebe was throwing a jealous fit, or if Adam had a friend over and it started to drizzle (the playdate rule was outdoors only, except for bathroom breaks and snacks and rain). Yet just as often, it was comforting. If Pammie closed her eyes during the day, as she often had to, what with Inka's busy night schedule, she did so with a sense of being able to keep track of what was going on in the house even as she dozed. And sometimes in the afternoons, when Pammie nursed Inka at the big table or tried to keep her awake while helping Adam with his homework, she found herself perversely, exhaustedly happy. Everything she did was worthwhile, and there were so many small victories. For example, though the kids still fought, it was no more than they used to. They ate three meals a day. Adam taught Phoebe how to play soccer. Inka learned to take both the bottle and the breast, and showed no signs of nipple confusion.

Pammie was contented by all this. She did regret not having someone to share it with. There was that background sadness, simple as the sky. And she missed considering, say, the deeper meaning of space in buildings. She missed higher thoughts in general. She remembered conversations she used to have with Andrea about the figured void, Le Corbusier's Unité d'Habitation, utopianism.

Yet, as time went on, she liked this house more and more. Maybe she felt returned by it to the small spaces of her childhood, and to its sounds and smells. That was one explanation. Or maybe anyone would love the way supper-making filled the conscious-ness of them all, here—the way they all heard together the *chop-chop* of vegetables being readied for cooking, the metallic *uuhch* of noodles being put in a pot, or the *sweesh* of rice being measured into the rice cooker. These were sounds that meant steam would be wafting everywhere soon enough, sweet with the smell of meat or sauce. No one needed to be told when supper was ready. The kids did need to be told to put what they were doing away, but they all knew why, and that the time had been coming; and when Pammie banged the cooking spoon on the lip of the frying pan that way, a double thump usually, to knock the food off, they knew it had come. They knew she would turn the heat off with a click, and open the refrigerator to get out some drinks, and they knew what she would say next. *Now. Set the table now, please. Now!*

It was absurd to be made happy by this small shared anticipa-tion. Before the table actually got set, there had to be an argument about whose turn it was. How could this make Pammie happy? But it did, even as it drove her batty. She liked her busy boredom, too, if only because it readied her for the moment when Adam presented Inka with a rattle shaped like a football, or when

Phoebe invented her own version of Duck, Duck, Goose: House, House, Home, this was called. You had to be a little bored to have those moments break over you the way they could. But if you sat waiting in a good dark night, they opened and opened like a brand of newfangled fireworks that lit the clouds, and the ground below, too, and all the faces turned upward, then fell with a sparkling rush right into your hands.

A VISIT

Pammie's mother did come once, and even cooked dinner, if only to show Pammie *what food should look like, in case you forgot.* It was hard to express gratitude of the appropriate level. Instead, Pammie took pictures of her mother cooking. There was Pammie's apron with a safety pin at the back of the neck to shorten the top half; there was her mother's bouffant of graying hair. Her mother was so short, and held herself so straight, that with one hand holding the pan still and the other stirring, she looked as though she were dancing with the stove. Of course, she did not dance, but there was a suggestion of gaiety to the cooking that Pammie wanted to remember—a sense that, at least with her back turned to the family, Pammie's mother was moved by something like love of it.

Pammie wanted to remember this particularly, since the act of actually dishing out the food seemed to renew her mother's annoyance at Pammie. Her mother frowned more and more deeply with each spoonful—causing Pammie's stomach to clench, even as she took note of how familiar both the clenching and the frowning were. Her mother had two creases between her eyebrows, perfectly parallel, one a little longer than the other; Pammie knew her mother would not have liked the extra length of that second crease if she could have seen it. *Making trouble,* she would have said, joking but not joking. *Just like you.* It was one of the few phrases Pammie knew in Chinese—*ma fan.* She did not know whether everyone defined it as her mother had. She only knew that in her mother's view, to stand out even in the smallest way, such as to draw attention, was to make trouble. A good child was one who did not trouble anyone—a child who understood the family's situation, the mother's situation, and who correspondingly kept herself small and edgeless.

Pammie's family was large and full of edges that snagged one's attention. A terrible, demanding bunch. Pammie's mother found Phoebe particularly trying—for example, right after dinner, when she poked a pair of knitting needles through the screen door.

—Look what she did. All the mosquitoes are now going to come right in the house, you watch and see. All summer long you people are going to be covered with bites.

Pammie could blame the children's behavior on Sven's leaving, but to her mother, it was clear that they had driven Sven away.

—Troublemakers, they are, she said. They do not know how to keep their father.

—I think fathers are supposed to stay no matter what, argued Pammie. Children are not supposed to have to work at keeping them. And didn't you always say Sven was good-for-nothing anyway?

—Not good for much, her mother conceded. I don't know why you married that art professor.

—I guess I should have asked myself whether art professors stuck around to raise their families, or whether they just took off after the children were born.

—You should have ask many things, said her mother. I just hope now you learned your lesson.

Pammie was not the only one to take pictures. Before she left, her mother took pictures, too, of Pammie's children, to add to her collection. She combed their hair and cleaned up their faces, and tried to angle her shots of Pammie's living room so that you could not see what a mess it was. Then she put on her coat, making comments that might, with some imagination, be construed as approval.

—Not that what you are dealing with is anything like what I did at your age. I was a newcomer to this country. I have no mother to lend me money. I have nobody to give me a house.

—Of course, said Pammie.

—You don't know what real hardship is.

—Very true, agreed Pammie.

—If you had asked me, I would have told you not to marry that Sven.

—I should have asked, said Pammie. Next time, I'll ask.

—Anyway, a mistake is a mistake, said her mother, finally softening. Why don't you come home, visit sometime? Or maybe some of your sisters can come to visit you. They would like to come visit, you know. They are just afraid.

—All right, said Pammie.

THE SPEED OF TRAFFIC ON MAIN STREET

Of course, the children and Pammie all missed Sven. They wondered about his circumstances when he did not call, which was often, and were angry at him when he visited, which was both much too often and not often enough. Pammie generally took advantage of his visits to walk around the block, or to have a cup of coffee in a local coffee shop, or to go take a shower at Andrea's or Dixie's house. Usually, she took Inka with her, even though Sven had expressed an interest in getting to know her.

—As far as she's concerned, you're a stranger, said Pammie.

—But how will I ever be a familiar if I never get to see her?

—You should have asked yourself that before you left.

At least he brought takeout when he came. With each visit, he left something different in the refrigerator; and Pammie found that she did look forward to seeing what it was—that opening the refrigerator helped her block out the sound of his steps receding. She tried not to watch him leave anymore. She tried not to wonder how he was doing, or whether he was developing a limp. She had thought, once, that she noticed a limp. Once, too, she had noticed someone in the car with him—a woman with short hair, or was it a slim man?

That was the same day Adam, as if reading her mind, came in with a paintbrush full of black paint.

—What are you doing? she asked.

—Oh, painting my windows, he said.

—Painting your windows? The glass or the wood?

—The glass.

—But Adam, we don't paint windows, you know that. Whatever gave you the idea you were allowed to paint your windows?

—I just didn't want to look out them anymore, he said.

The great irony, of course, was that Sven would have liked to hear how much more Pammie shrugged off now, having no choice. She did not yell at Adam, for example, but quietly helped him clean up; just as she did not worry about going to Adam's infamous soccer games—he obviously went alone. How simple some things had become. When Inka was old enough to go to preschool, she went, so that Pammie could start looking for another job. They had spent most of their savings by then, so the decision was clear.

She started to do things at the children's school, too, when she could. Not that she was thinking about trying to meet somebody new, exactly. She was thinking more about making some friends besides Andrea and Dixie, her lifelines. But it was hard—she felt so much older and more careworn than the people around her, living the way she did. Though they were kind to her, they by and large talked about things of which she had no knowledge. Shops, vacation packages, Supreme Court decisions. They criticized the principal, the speed of traffic on Main Street, the sorts of movies shown at the movie house. Slowly, she began to talk about these things, too; then more fluently; and yet there was a part of her that remained strange. Still she tried. She bought her first Lycra anything, a pair of leggings. Whatever else she had lost in the last few years, she at least had her legs. Shopkeepers said she looked like a college student, that she could pass for someone's au pair, that it was hard to believe she was a mother of three, especially when she put her hair up. She bought herself a pair of platform mules, furthering this pleasant illusion. She shopped in the natural-foods grocery store. She fed the kids dried fruit, grains. She balked at wheat grass, however, and allowed the deep mystery that was spirulina to remain a deep mystery. When she joined the diversity committee, it was in the hopes of finding a place in the bright town she had actually been living in for some years now.

THE ADVENT OF CARVER

She had this expectation: that life would go on more or less as it had; that her largest drama was behind her.

Then one day she helped organize the children of color lunch, only to happen upon the man in Phoebe's classroom; and not much later, he was in her house—enormous Carver, dwarfing her kitchen, complaining about the scale of Colonial architecture. Pammie felt as though she had discovered, over by the cupboard, a false wall. It was as if she had pushed, unknowingly, on a secret spring; suddenly Carver stepped forward, replete with stories and opinions. How lilliputian the colonists were! That was one. He sipped a beer as he talked, his hand so large that it engulfed the can; almost all Pammie could see of it was its gold metal top. The architecture made you feel the colonists' size, he said. It made you feel what pale little types they were, easily tuckered out by snow shoveling. As for himself—Carver said he used to work on a sugar plantation on Kauai. He told her about losing his finger in the fields, cutting cane—he was just lucky the rats didn't eat it, he said. He told her about having it stitched back on; he told her about the problem of the rats in general, and about rat poison. He told her about planting the eyes of the cane, and about burning the fields before the harvest. He told her about losing his new job, as a cane-truck driver. That was good money while it lasted, he said. But sugar, the world market, the First World, the Third. At least he had lived outside the plantation before. There were families who had not lived on their own for generations; they didn't know how to find work, they didn't know how to find housing. Yet they were turned out by the hundreds all the same. He told her about realizing himself how small the islands were—about realizing how even the longest roads were circles, leading nowhere. A bellboy job only convinced him that tourism was indeed whorism. What sort of life was it to yearn endlessly, achingly for the Japanese to visit in their former glorious numbers? Pammie shook her head, half dazed, agreeing: It was no life. Neither was Carver cut out for the low ceilings of government work. He saw clearly that he was going to have to go back to school—he had dropped out after two years—and was considering how he would do so. In the meantime, he squatted on a beach in Molokai with a group of other ex–plantation workers. Some of them had turned Hawaiian separatists.

—It was cheap, he offered. Every now and then, we threw rocks at tourist buses. When we were all working, you could think whatever you wanted, but now you had to watch which way your tongue curled. You couldn't ask whether Hawaii could really survive without the United States. You couldn't ask how we could make do without tourism. So I didn't ask. But everybody knew that I wondered. *How come you so haolefied,* they'd say in pidgin, and give me the stink eye. A haole, you know, is a white person. *You moddah faddah wen fo live too long on da mainland,* they said. And of course, it is true that both my parents spent too many years here, before taking us kids back home to Hawaii.

He stopped to fasten his gaze on her; she felt herself caught within it; and for a moment, she wondered what Sven would think of Carver. She knew what he would say about Carver's finger.

It was the odd incidental detail that got you. We are never immune to such pleasures.

Could it have been the penile suggestion that piqued you?

But what would Sven say about Carver's presence—about his soft, sure voice, about his monk's face, about his ever-deliberate manner? His gestures unfolded in sequence, like a ripple. First he would settle his eyebrows slowly, as now; then he would nod; and only then would he smile his gentle, spreading smile. In this, as in all things, he took his time.

—Then I got this job as an au pair for a family with seven boys. They flew me here, paid my health insurance, gave me a car to drive. No one else would work for them. They were desperate.

—Will you go back?

—Depends on what grows here, he said.

PAMMIE LETS HIM BUILD

Carver played basketball with Adam, teaching him how to put backspin on the ball when he shot from the foul line.

—*L, I,* Say good-bye, he instructed. You've got to hold the ball so the lines run horizontal. It's all in the fingertips.

He taught Phoebe how to draw a foul.

—Foul! Foul! she would yell at Adam with the vindicated air of someone who has learned to express a core truth of her world.

Inka, meanwhile, would happily echo her sister from her seat atop Carver's shoulders.

—Foul! she would say; and other times, Basket!

Carver would steady her with his left hand while dribbling up to the basket with his right. Then he would stop and give her the ball.

—Inka shoot! she would cry, dumping the ball into the net. Inka three-pointer!

And Pammie, whose own shooting seemed to be improving these days, what with all the practice, would laugh.

Who would have turned him away? More and more, he spent evenings with the family, talking. He told them all about Kauai, the most indomitable of the Hawaiian islands. He told them how in the old days warriors would paddle over from Oahu in their outrigger canoes and attack, only to have the Kauai warriors laugh, catching the enemy spears in their bare hands. He made the children candy leis. He taught them to salt their pineapple to make it taste sweeter. He introduced them to Spam, and to pidgin.

—Ono! they cried as they ate. Dat Spam so ono!

—No talk stink! they told one another. No make li' dat!

He told them stories about the family with seven boys: How the boys had turned the living room into a gymnasium, complete with trampoline. How the boys had turned the dining room into a hall of lizards. How six of the boys had taken up the drums at one time or another, but one boy, the violin. Carver had worked for that family for five years; they had sent him to school in gratitude. This was how he eventually ended up assisting in Phoebe's class.

—And how I met you. He gazed unabashedly at Pammie.

Pammie wasn't sure what she thought about that. But when the time came for Carver to find a new home—his current official residence was on a friend's couch—Pammie agreed to let him renovate her garage into a suite for himself. He had built many things before, it turned out, and they came up with a wonderful plan: to leave the old garage door in place, only replacing the glass with obscured glass for privacy, so that, from the street side, the garage would look as it always had. The back, south-facing wall, though, was to be bumped out with a greenhouselike porch, so that, overall, the garage room would have a cavelike feel of deep shade fronted with intense light. The shady part of the garage room was not unbroken; diffuse light was to come from the old garage windows, and from a small existing side window. But the overall experience of vivid contrast was supposed to remind Carver of the tropics; and so deeply pleased was he about this idea, when Pammie first unveiled it, that he laughed and quite uncharacteristically suggested a little kitsch: bamboo on the walls, straw mats on the floor.

—The complete South Seas experience! Coconut-shell lamps! laughed Pammie. She added a rain gutter whose downspouts would pour over the front porch.

—Waterfalls! she said.

Would a true South Seas experience include plumbing? Pammie thought they should go ahead and put it in, seeing as how the whole family was already sharing the one bathroom in the house. It was going to be expensive, what with the digging involved; but Pammie said, as airily as she could manage, Never mind the expense.

—It's a home improvement, she said.

—You should think it over. It might not make sense.

They were quiet for a moment.

—You're right. It makes no sense, said Pammie.

Still, the next day, Carver brought her a bag of Dragon's Well tea. For this was one of the many things he knew about, besides carpentry—how to drink tea. He showed her the whole ceremony, which a friend of his from Singapore had taught him. He showed Pammie how to pour water over the special clay pot to warm it up; there was a little slotted tray into which the excess water dripped. He showed her, too, the bamboo spatula used to scoop the tea, and how you inserted it, then flipped your wrist a little so as not to break any leaves. He showed her how you steeped the tea, and how you tasted the tea from cups barely bigger than a thimble. It was all very beautiful and peaceful; yet as Pammie sipped, all she could think was, How precious! A little Chinese-style gazebo of an experience. She tried not to think. She tried to listen to the clink of the pottery and to Carver's clear, explaining voice. She tasted the tea, blowing on its surface to cool it down. The steam blew back up into her face; she could feel the muscles under her eyes relax. *No thinking.* She closed her eyes, pretending not to notice how very close to her Carver was sitting. Their knees touched; neither of them moved. Instead, they allowed themselves simply to adjoin each other for a while, breathing.

THE SPACES MADE POSSIBLE

Authenticity—that was the sort of thing Carver talked about over the weeks that followed. Also other things, to which Pammie could hear Sven reply, *Nonsense!* Still, she listened carefully. It was the talk of the nineties, of a new generation—how she had been wifed, how she had been fetishized, how she had been viewed as Orientalia. How she had been sabotaged, how she ought to be outraged. But she was not outraged, not yet. For now she was merely interested, being too full of wondering: Where would all this lead? The knee-touching had naturally opened into other activities. Now she watched Carver setting up his sawhorses in the backyard, and her very body seemed a question. Would they stay lovers? Already she wanted him forever, the warm and easy expanse of him, the ever-ready impulse of him. He had smooth, sensitive skin like her own, easily sent into goose bumps; that one stiff finger; a mischief-making tongue. How rounded he made her feel, how sensate and pliant and full of destinations. He was physically inspired by the smallest patch of sun—never mind if it be amid the clutter of the ki*** en table; yet his unbridled instinct was to meet her and be met, more than to overtake her. Intellectually, he was less respectful. Intellectually, he could be a tidal wave. Yet having learned, at long last, to withstand Sven, Pammie found she could withstand this one, too, easily. It was only a matter of inhabiting, with a certain adamance, herself. As for Carver's habitation—would he one day move into the house? And what was Sven going to say when he found out? Should she ask for a divorce? Sometimes she envisioned herself working in the garage, which had mysteriously sprouted skylights and become her studio. The light was distinctly cool. What did that mean?

Sometimes, too, she thought back to the day she organized the children of color lunch, and how, not a week after that, at the school fall fair, she wrote a letter to a fortune-telling pineapple. Over and over she saw her children in the arts and crafts tent, making a present for her. Adam had told her to go away; also that he needed Inka. That meant hand- or footprints of some sort, Pammie imagined. And so she wandered over to the stand next to the tent, where there stood a gaudily decorated cardboard refrigerator box with a kind of palm tree growing out of it. There was no one attending the stand, but as she paused in front of it, a note emerged from a slot in its front.

Help me! The fortune-telling pineapple needs business. Fifty cents buys you life wisdom and happiness. You have only to say who you are and what you have become.

She laughed. A clipboard with paper and pen hung from the side of the box.

Dear Pineapple,

I have, against all odds, become an adult. I thought that adulthood was something that emanated from the inside. But now I find that it has more to do with the outside pressing in. It ought not to be a shock, finding oneself with responsibilities. But it is a shock all the same.

The pineapple shook when she gave it the note. A minute later, an answer emerged.

You cannot imagine what my life is like either, it read. *What do I really know, a tropical fruit like me? And yet I try to make a few things up, for there comes a day when people stop asking.*

True enough. Pammie deposited her fifty cents into the slot. Another piece of paper emerged.

Are you married? Pineapples make good friends.

She wrote:

I could use a good friend. But what does that have to do with marriage?

Said a third slip:

You once made someone a _____ wife. Fill in the blank.

But Pammie did not fill in the blank. She laughed and walked away, a surprising spring in her step. She knew who the pineapple was, of course—that man in the classroom, the monk-faced one with the finger injury; the man whom she would know, soon, as

Carver. And she could sense without even trying that soon, soon she would be hearing the story of that finger. Soon, soon she would be enlightened, as well—on the subject of her retrograde marriage, and so on. Looking back, it seemed to her that she could feel it coming, the force of revelation that lay packed up in that man.

But did she really foresee it all? Perhaps she had only experienced a small moment of foreboding.

Today she shrugged, in any case, and allowed herself the possibility of clairvoyance. For the fact was that she had had moments of strange clarity before; also, that she had turned away. How was it that her men tended to come so well equipped? Anatomically, of course, but with truths, too, big truths. She had smiled as she turned. She was interested in truths.

But it was possible—this was her truth—to be living too much life. She knew this now, how life could come at you. All at once, and without respite.

Her children were in a tent. Outside was a day, not as tremendous as any she'd ever seen, but tremendous enough, and clear. It was the kind of red and yellow fall day that people drove from faraway brown towns to come see; the kind of day when the world feels full of street corners, because at every one you gape like a tourist at the heart-stopping spectacle which is your very own world, without chlorophyll. She meant to go lie down for ten minutes in an open field. If something more was going to happen to her—if she was going to fall fatally in love again, for example—she at least wanted to watch some clouds drift before she did.

For now that she was indeed an adult, she understood no space so well as eventless space. In architecture school, people had talked of *poches*—the nondescript pockets left, for example, by a circular room inscribed in a square. Enigmatic spaces, they were; useless places; places of no identity at all. And yet how they enlivened the spaces they made possible.

ACKNOWLEDGMENTS

Many thanks to my fellow mothers, whose countless acts of kindness and understanding made this book possible. Heartfelt thanks, too, to my husband, David O'Connor; to my editor, Ann Close; to my agent, Maxine Groffsky; and to my most excellent readers, Margot Livesey, Jayne Anne Phillips, Allegra Goodman, Ha Jin, Katrina Kenison, Dawn Delbanco, and Maryann Thompson.

ALSO BY GISH JEN

MONA IN THE PROMISED LAND

In this ebullient and inventive novel, Gish Jen restores multiculturalism from high concept to a fact of life. At least that's what it becomes for teenage Mona Chang, who in 1968 moves with her newly prosperous family to Scarshill, New York, where the Chinese have become "the new Jews." What could be more natural than for Mona to take this literally—even to the point of converting?

As Mona attends temple "rap" sessions and falls in love (with a nice Jewish boy who lives in a tepee), Jen introduces us to one of the most charming and sweet-spirited heroines in recent fiction, a girl who can wisecrack with perfect aplomb even when she's organizing the help in her father's pancake house. On every page of *Mona in the Promised Land*, Gish Jen sets our received notions spinning with a wit as dry as a latter-day Jane Austen's.

"A shining example of a multicultural message delivered with the wit and bite of art. . . . Gish Jen creates a particular world where dim sum is as American as apple pie."

—*Los Angeles Times*

Fiction/0-679-77650-8

VINTAGE CONTEMPORARIES
Available at your local bookstore, or call toll-free to order:
1-800-793-2665 (credit cards only).